# MISTRESS OF DARKNESS: STORIES OF THE MACABRE (Volume 1)

By

Del Gibson

HORRORific Publishing

HORRORific Productions Ltd

61 Bridge Street, Kington, Herefordshire HR5 3DJ



First published in Great Britain 2025

The paperback edition first published in 2025



Edited by Colin C Martin

A catalogue record for this book is available from the British Library

Paperback ISBN: 978-1-0684637-1-6

Beth's attempt at a fresh start leads to disaster in the after world. A seemingly standard paranormal investigation uncovers dark family secrets. A youth group's camping expedition awakens something in the wilderness...

Step into a world of shadows, dark desires and otherworldly realms with the debut anthology from New Zealand author Del Gibson.

## Contents

I dedicate this book to my husband Benjamin; my soulmate, and our children for your ongoing love and support throughout my writing journey. I couldn't have done this without you all.

**Introduction and Special Thanks:**

This anthology is my debut book. Something which has been brewing away inside my head for several years, and finally here it is. Thank you to everyone who helped me along the way. I would like to give special thanks to Colin Martin for always believing in me. Your advice and encouragement have got me through some really tough times. I am forever grateful to you for that.

# One Lost Soul

I was standing at the boot of my SUV, collecting my belongings, and as I glanced up, I saw a woman standing at my bedroom window. I blinked and she was gone. I should have left then but I didn't.

Do you ever wish you had listened to your instincts? You know that gut punch that warns you something isn't right? It shivered right through me, but I brushed it off. There was no going back, and nothing to go back to anyway.

This would be my new beginning, a fresh start away from pushy parents and an abusive ex-boyfriend.

After slamming the boot shut and with the last box in hand, and wrestling with a bag of groceries, I climbed the stairs to my new abode on the second story.

When I found this apartment on a realtor's website, I paid the deposit immediately, because rental properties are fairly hard to find in the CBD. I was fortunate this one had recently become available. The photographs showed a small tidy flat, with a good-sized bathroom and included a bathtub. The only bedroom was sunny and bright, boasting a walk-in wardrobe. Although the décor was a little outdated, I was happy with it, and the fact it came fully furnished was an added bonus.

The complex appeared to be well maintained, and the apartments identical to each other. There's a staircase at either end of the building, and the terraces leading to the flats overlook a large front garden, with a small pool. I was surprised it was quite a lot cheaper than some of the other properties I'd searched online.

It had been a full-on day unpacking boxes and rearranging the existing furniture. Exhaustion overcame me, desperate for sleep, I climbed into bed. That is when I first heard the scratching coming from within the walls. I jumped out of bed in fright, flicked on the light switch, but for some reason it didn't work. I tried again, to no avail. I followed the scratching around in the darkness, believing it was rats or some other rodents making their home inside the walls. I remember thinking there might be an infestation, perhaps that explained the cheaper rent.

I gave up and tried to sleep, slightly confused and a little disturbed. I tossed and turned all night, so my first night sleeping in my new flat was fractured.

The persistent scratching continued for a week or so, until they turned into little knocks and taps all over the flat, from inside the cupboards, wardrobe, the walls and on the internal doors. It continued for weeks on end. I couldn't sleep, my appetite was completely obsolete, and I couldn't tell you the last time I had a shower. Then the knocking and tapping suddenly stopped one night, and the silence was wonderful. However, I could feel a high tension and pressure building, like it does right before a storm.

Then I started to notice that items were disappearing and being moved around my flat. It really started to bother me. I began to think that someone was getting into the apartment somehow and was intentionally trying to mess with my mind.

I decided it was time to meet the neighbours. Perhaps they would know what was going on in my home. I'd been here for weeks and hadn't come across a single person. I knocked upon every door in the complex, but no one answered. I thought it was a little weird, then again, they might all be at work or study. It wasn't long after that, everything turned to shit.

The shadows came. I began to see them everywhere, I thought I was going crazy! They'd be lurking in the hallway, I'd glance them in the mirrors, that I eventually covered with sheets. Lying in bed, I could hear them whispering in the darkness, while I lay there shivering in fear.

One night I woke to find someone standing at the foot of my bed. In fright, I turned on the bedside lamp, but the figure had gone. When they started moving furniture, opening and shutting cupboards, slamming closed the internal doors, I knew I was out of my depth. But there was no one to tell. My cell phone battery was dead and I couldn't find my charger, so there wasn't a chance for me to call anyone for help.

One morning, I woke to find the table stacked with items from the pantry. The cans were piled on top of one another, almost reaching the ceiling. The glasses, cups and crockery from the cupboards, were also stacked precariously in the same way. As I stood in the doorway, confused and scared, I heard banging at the front door. When I went to answer it, a little old lady was standing there being sprinkled with raindrops.

"Hello," I said.

"Yes, hello there, isn't it a beautiful day? I love the rain," said the strange woman in a quiet, gentle voice.

We stood there for a moment staring each other down: Her eyes were as black as coal. I was holding the door between us, as a glacial shiver made its way down my spine. If this lady was a door knocker trying to sell me something, we were off to an awkward start. Her silence became alarming and ominous, and I had a horrid feeling that there was something not quite right with this person.

"Can I help you?" I asked. Thinking it must be a neighbour, I softened my fear.

"Well dear. That is the million-dollar question," she replied.

"Are you looking for someone?" I asked as my voice cracked.

"No, I am not looking for anyone, it's you I came to see."

Her face changed suddenly, she was no longer quiet and old, she looked menacing. Her eyes rolled into the back of her head as she inched her way closer towards me.

"Let me in, dear,' she said, 'I have something for you!"

My survival mode kicked in, so I slammed the door shut in her face. In a state of utter shock, I fell backwards. She stood there slamming her forehead into the glass panel in the door, repeatedly, leaving a bloody mush on the glass. I scrambled back into the dining-room, only to discover all of the items were gone from the table. I rushed around searching through the cupboards and the pantry; everything was back to their rightful place.

After several long agonising minutes, her insistent knocking at the door stopped suddenly. By that stage I had had enough, so I grabbed my keys, wallet and cell phone, thinking I would charge it in the car. I peeked out of the lounge window, hiding myself behind the curtain. The old woman was gone. At the front door I was baffled, the blood was no longer there on the glass.

I closed the door behind me and started to make my way down the staircase to the carpark. But when I finally got to the bottom, the staircase didn't stop, they kept going down. I didn't have time to ponder this; I just kept running down the steps. Every time I thought I had made it to the bottom, I would end up back in front of my apartment, Number 23. After a while of doing this and getting nowhere, I was shattered.

Back inside, I sunk down on the couch and cried. I remember thinking I was stuck there forever, that it was hopeless. There was no escaping this hell hole of a building. I tried to leave every single day for weeks; it became habitual. But the same thing happened, over and over. The staircase had no end, and the knocking, scratching and furniture moving around the rooms had increased. The shadow people watched me from the darkest corners of the rooms.

One cold night the power went out, plunging me into darkness. I found some candles and a box of matches in a kitchen draw, but soon enough they all burned down to nothing. Hours turned into days and days turned into weeks. I stayed inside my flat for months. Every now and then a new person would arrive, begging me to let them in. Around and around my life went on. My days got twisted, everyday blurring into the next. I'd lost all concept of time.

Then one day, I woke to find people in my flat. I could hear their muffled talk through the walls. I hadn't heard voices in so long, it startled me. They slowly walked around from room to room. I didn't know who they were, or why they were there. I was so scared that I quickly hid in the bathroom so they wouldn't find me. When I got sick of that and curiosity got the better of me, I started following them around. When I entered the lounge, loud alarms screamed, it was so brutal that I had to cover my ears. Glaring bright white lights blared at me. I ran from the room and hid under my bed.

"Is there someone here with us? Come out and talk, if you come near one of these devices, we will be able to hear you. Can you make a noise, so we know where you are?"

I decided I would, because I hadn't spoken to anyone for god knows how long – it had felt like years and years. I knocked on the wall in the hallway and they all came running, there were three people, a woman and two men. Due to my instinctual fear of men, I tried to stay as far away from them as possible, but they stalked me through the apartment.

"Who is here with us? What is your name?" the woman asked.

With the small amount of energy I had, I answered.

"Elizabeth."

Hearing my voice come out of the little box she was holding, intrigued me.

"How long have you been here, Elizabeth? Can I call you that or would you prefer to be called Liz or Beth?"

I always hated that name, Elizabeth; it made me feel old.

"Beth," I answered.

Once again, I was enthralled by the box that said my words. But I started to become upset, because these people were intruding in my home, and I still had no idea why they were here. How the hell did they get inside? Suddenly a loud beeping sound screamed from one of the devices, and the lights on it flickered from green to red. I was mesmerised and somewhat excited by this.

"Wow, she is here right in front of us. Keep asking questions Michelle, she seems to want to speak to you. After what happened here, to her, it doesn't surprise me."

*A long-ago memory entered my mind*…There was a man inside my apartment who had done something horrendous to me.

The memory dissipated when the woman's voice broke through the silence.

"Beth, how long have you been here?"

My energy was draining fast, so I used one of the devices to give me enough strength to answer.

"Ten years."

"Who killed you Beth?"

I didn't want to say it, but I did.

"Simon."

"It really is her! She knows who did it. Simon Klass."

Hearing that name made me angry. I screwed my eyes closed as my entire body trembled. When I opened them again, the flat looked different. Old and abandoned. What the hell was happening? On the shelf I found a broken bowl and I launched it across the room. They jumped from the mouldy dilapidated couches in fright, standing in the middle of the room, looking around, confused.

"Michelle, you scared her. Here, I have a question," said the fat man.

"Beth, my name is John. Do you know you are dead?"

I was beyond anger, and something fierce was building inside of me.

"Get out!" I screamed with all of my might, but it came out a garbled mess of noise.

The tall man with a beard, picked up a device with a bright light and a small TV screen attached to it. I had never seen anything like it before. I was curious, so I wandered over to get a better look. Then I scrambled away when the lady started talking again.

"You can show yourself on the device in Tony's hand. It is called an SLS camera and we can see you if you stand in front of it."

It didn't make any sense to me, none of it did, but I decided to play along. I stood on the top of the bookshelf in the living room, and although it was broken, I managed to do it.

"There she is. Look, she's on the shelf."

Hearing this, I darted away – making loud noises as I stomped along the hallway, knocking on the walls, kicking the doors. I was about to try to smash the already cracked mirror, when I was rudely interrupted.

"Did you hear that?" one of the men asked.

I slammed the bathroom door shut, hoping to scare them out of my flat.

"Get out! Leave!" I yelled, as I shoved the woman, nearly knocking her over.

"What the hell? Something just pushed me and the devices are going nuts! Look at the REM pod, she must be touching it. The K2 meter is spiking to red too," she said aghast. "Beth, we are here to help you. We can free you from here, you don't have to stay here anymore."

I didn't trust them, because I didn't know their intentions. I remember thinking that perhaps they could help me leave the building for good. So I hovered around them waiting to see what they would do next.

"Beth, I feel you are still mad about what happened to you. What he did to you was terrible. But he is no longer here, he is dead now."

*Then I remembered...*I was struggling with the last of my gear from the car, when a man approached me and asked if he could help. I noticed he came from the flat beneath mine. I gladly accepted. He took the heavy box from me, I carried the groceries, and together we entered my apartment.

"Where should I put this box?" he asked.

"Just in the bedroom on the bed please. That would be great."

As I fluffed around in the kitchen, packing away the shopping, I noticed he still hadn't come out of my bedroom, so I went looking for him. When I entered, he was standing in my closet, going through what little clothes I had hung up.

"What are you doing?" I asked, giving him a fright.

"Nothing, just wondering if your wardrobe is the same size as mine."

I didn't believe him because he had a pair of my stockings wrapped around his hands. Instinctively I recognised there was danger, but I didn't want to inflame the situation, so I laughed it off, not wanting him to see how scared I actually was at that moment.

"Thank you for your help. How rude of me I don't even know your name," I commented.

"Simon Klass, lovely to meet you. Are you sure I can't help you unpack? Four hands are better than two." He chuckled too loudly to be genuine.

"I'm all good, thank you. I will let you get on with your day. Thanks heaps for your help, Simon," I said, trying to push him gently towards the door.

Suddenly, he grabbed me, and with my own stockings he strangled me to death. Then he did other things to me I wish I could erase forever. After that he set the apartment building on fire. When they found my remains, I stood there crying. It wasn't fair, my life ending like that.

I snapped out of my reverie when the woman started talking again.

"Beth, if you need help to leave here, please knock on the wall, or make a sound."

I had no energy left, so I drained the battery from one of their cameras. With all of my remaining strength, I screamed through the device, "Help me!"

So they did. I watched as they walked from room to room, splashing water on the damaged walls. I could hear them praying as they languished in my bedroom, spreading smoke from a bunch of sticks they held in their hands. The woman made the sign of the cross in every doorway, banishing any spirits who weren't supposed to be there. One of the men splashed more of the water on all the smashed windows and the ruined floorboards in every room. At the front door, the woman was saying she was opening a doorway for me to go through.

"Follow the light Beth. You will find peace there. You can move on if that is what you want. Just follow the light, and at the end you will be free," she explained in a soft voice.

I trusted her, so I moved slowly over to the front door, as they stood in the hallway watching on their devices. There was a light, and I followed it to the end of the tunnel, not knowing quite what to expect. Someone was walking towards me, and she seemed very familiar.

"Hello my darling, Beth. You made it. Come with me sweetheart and I will take you home."

I hadn't heard my mother's sweet voice for over twenty years. When finally I melted into her arms, the tears fell hard. She held my hand as we walked away from the old, abandoned apartment complex.

I was finally free from the hell I had been living in, roaming the place where I'd been murdered – trying to escape. I didn't even know that I was dead.

# Searching for Lucy

When we arrive at the Wallace's estate, darkness is setting in, big black dusty clouds surround the property as we drive down the long winding driveway with conifer trees standing sentinel on either side. When finally, the house makes its appearance, I am astonished at the size of the sprawling mansion. We are here to conduct a paranormal investigation, searching for Lucy Wallace who practically vanished into thin air. The Mother had reached out to us yesterday.

I park in front of the mansion, and we sit there in awe for a while taking in its opulence. The stonework looks ancient, almost giving it the impression of a castle – it must be very old. Hundreds of windows stare down upon us, little ones and large ones, and some round ones that look like eyes. The structure is three stories high.

"You didn't tell me we were coming here!" Matt our camera man exclaims in exasperation.

"Well I didn't want to spook you; I know how much you hate the guy, but we have to help his family. It is what we do Matt, you know it," I simply say.

"But he is a monumental pain in the butt, a billionaire with a chip on his shoulders. The last time I ran into him, he was screaming at a waitress in a café calling her all sorts of derogatory names. Just because she didn't bring his Latte to him fast enough," Matt huffs in the passenger seat beside me, crossing his arms over his chest.

"No matter what you think about this man, remember he just lost his daughter," I seethe at Matt's insensitivity.

"Matt," Ian breathes out a sigh of frustration. "You always have something to complain about. They need our help. We never turn people away, no matter who it is. You know that!"

"So, what happened to the little girl? I saw something pop up on my news feed, but I didn't have time to read it," Ian comments.

"The Mother, Bella, told me that her and three-year-old Lucy were playing outside in the garden. She says she popped inside for a minute to get some water but when she went back outside Lucy was gone. She seems to be a nice lady, but obviously on the brink of a breakdown."

"Well did they find her, Julia?" Ian asks.

"No. Obviously or we wouldn't be here! They have no idea where she is. The police have searched everywhere, as well as hundreds of volunteers. They brought in a helicopter and a K9 unit – two dogs for search and rescue and two cadaver dogs – they took them through the house too, but nothing eventuated. It's been nearly a month, and the parents are frantically desperate to find her. So that is why we are here. Hopefully we can find her through our methods. The police have officially called off the search."

A shiver courses through me as we unpack the cases holding our equipment from the boot of the car. I feel eyes watching us.

Suddenly, the front door opens and Mr and Mrs Wallace come down the steps to greet us.

"Matt, what's the difference between Michael Jackson and Casper?" Ian whispers.

"Hell Ian, I don't know."

"One is white and scares young children, and the other is a ghost," Ian tries to hide his giggle, but it escapes the edges.

"Shut up you two!" I mutter under my breath.

After brief introductions and handshakes, we are directed to enter the house. We follow the Wallace's into a spacious room filled to the brim with antiquities. Long velvet drapes close us in, and Tiffany lamps spread a soft amber glow around the room.

"Thank you for coming at such short notice," Bella says, sniffing back her pain. "I have asked a friend of ours, Mary Clay, a clairvoyant, to assist you tonight. I hope you don't mind?"

She begins to cry, and her husband pats her back, slowly moving her into the chair around a beautifully crafted table. Sitting at the end is Mary Clay. Over the years, we have bumped into each other at festivals and fairs, but have never been formally introduced. She acknowledges us with a glance, then closes her eyes; I think she is praying.

We begin to unpack our equipment. The main instrument we are going to use tonight is my one-hundred-year-old Ouija board; it has been passed down the family. My Grandmother, Aunty Ollie and my Mother were all Wiccan. Me, not so much. I prefer to communicate with spirits using tools and instruments, and sometimes, but not usually, we use my Ouija board.

"Matt, did you hear about the ghost who got put in prison?"

"Ian, shut up," I hiss.

"He was charged with possession."

I gently kick him in the shin, it shuts him up immediately. I know he does it to lighten the mood, but it can be very annoying. He also knows it wears thin after a while and I am forever trying to keep him focused on the job.

"What are those things you have there?" Mr Able Wallace asks, with a petulant tone seeping into his voice.

As I remove each item from their cases, I explain their functions, placing them upon an exquisite side table nearest to me.

"This is a Ouija board, we use it to communicate with spiritual entities. This is a K2 meter, it senses energy, and it flashes from green to red if there is a spirit nearby. We also have this, it is a REM pod device.

It senses energy and gages temperature changes. If an entity touches the aerial on top, it will flash to green and it will set off an alarm."

I start to unload the trigger case. When I pull out the teddy bear, I hear Bella exhale a long-anguished breath.

"What is that for? Why do you have a teddy bear?" she asks, clearly unsettled.

"Well, these are called trigger toys. The teddy bear asks questions to any spirit who touches it. It tends to attract children; they are very curious about it, and because some haven't seen a toy in years, it comforts them – making it easier to communicate. But I am not saying Lucy is in spirit, it is just another tool we use. Much like these ones."

I bring out a handful of cat ball toys, to deflect the conversation from Lucy. "These light up when a spirit touches them." I turn them on and they light up in my hand.

I stop talking when I notice Able Wallace's eyes glaze over with boredom.

"Anyway, this is our best bet at investigations." Ian takes over. "It is an Ovilus device, a spirit box, it picks out words that are already registered into the device and speaks them. Usually we get clear responses."

"Bella...," I begin to say, but I am rudely interrupted by Able Wallace.

"Excuse me miss, whatever your name is, I would prefer you use our titles please, we do not know you or your team of ghostbusters. I find it completely disrespectful that you use our given names."

"Okay...sorry. Ummm...Mrs Wallace, usually we will get a much better response if we can use some of Lucy's items as trigger objects. Do you think that will be okay?" I ask, red faced, the heat making my skin irritable – much like my mood.

She looks at me with a grimace on her face and diamond tears in her eyes.

"Yes of course, if it will help. What do you suggest?"

"Well, does she have a favourite toy? A special blanket, or item of clothing? A piece of jewellery, perhaps? Anything to connect with her guardian angels," I say.

I am very careful to use present tense, as past tense could infer she is dead. I am hoping we can find her alive, that she has merely wandered off.

"Just give me a minute," she says, pushing away from the table and leaving the room.

The silence is deafening. If a pin dropped it would have sounded like an explosion. Mr Wallace's face is like thunder as he stares daggers at us. Mary Clay has her head in her hands. Ian and Matt are setting up the devices and positioning two static cameras around the table.

"Matt, who do ghosts worship? Boo, DUH..."

"For the love of God, be quiet," right then I could have strangled him to death.

Bella returns holding an armful of items. She sits back at the table and spreads each of them out in front of us.

"This is her favourite doll, Isabella – she named it after me. It was last year's Christmas present," she says, as she pampers its head absentmindedly. "Her fairy dress, she loves this, especially the wings." She sniffs in the scent left over from her missing child. "Boo Bear, her Grandparents brought him into the hospital the day she was born, and she has slept with him every night ever since. When Lucy went missing, she was playing with Boo Bear in the garden, I found him in the mud." Her tears splatter onto its tiny furry body.

Bella hugs it into her, and bawls giant sobs that practically engulf her. The entire time, Mary Clay keeps her eyes closed. When we are all seated at the table, excluding Matt who is operating the cameras, she suddenly speaks, startling me.

"Spirit, all mighty Father, heavenly guides and angels, may you please protect us all as we conduct this session. We are gathered here to find Lucy May Wallace. There are devices here that you can use to communicate with us. We are not here to hurt anyone, we just need to know what happened to Lucy, and where we can find her." She folds her hands into the prayer position.

Bella is softly weeping as Mary Clay talks about her missing daughter, and Able Wallace doesn't comfort her, he is distant, staring mesmerized at the Ouija board laid out on the table.

"What I want everyone to do is place two fingers of each hand tentatively on the planchette in the middle of the board. Now there are rules here," I say, pointedly. "This can be very dangerous if it is done incorrectly. Never let your fingers leave the planchette at any time, no matter what happens, no matter how scared you are by the responses. We cannot finish the session without moving it to the goodbye point on the board. Essentially, we are opening a portal to communicate with spirit. If this ends without spirit allowing us to say goodbye, there will be dire consequences. Does everyone understand?"

They all agree, and we each place our fingers upon the old wooden planchette. It is smooth to the touch. Instantly, I feel a vibration of energy tingling through my fingers, and the room is charged with tension. Our devices are switched on, and the cameras are rolling.

"Is there anyone here with us who would like to communicate? Please come through and speak into one of the devices, or use our fingers on this board to answer," I say confidently.

Something bumps hard against the table. Mary Clay's eyes fly open, and in the ambient lamp light, her eyes look like they are glowing – she pierces me with them, somewhat scaring me. When finally she speaks again, her voice is deep and gravelly.

"Come closer, I can sense you. Who is here with us?" she implores.

Through the Ovilus device, a voice replies, "I am here!" startling everyone, and the planchette starts to move slowly across the Ouija board.

"What is your name?" I demand, my skin crawling, the sensation always feels like cobwebs covering my head.

Suddenly, whomever it is with us begins to spell out letters on the board. D. E. V. I. L. A gasp escapes my mouth; my skin is prickling with goosebumps. The others make their own astonished noises, thankfully no one lets go of the planchette.

"Oh my God," screams Bella.

"This is preposterous," Able Wallace yells across the table.

"Able, please. Let one of us ask the questions, we know what we are doing." Mary Clay cuts him down quickly. "Spirit, you are not the devil. Who are you? I command you to tell us."

The planchette begins a steady crawl across the board, when suddenly the REM pods spread around the room, scream their alarms. I look over at it and the lights are going spastic.

"D. E. V. I. L."

Something in the room crashes to the ground.

"Oh my God, that's our wedding portrait." Bella shrieks in fright.

Glass and frame shatter upon the floor, and in horror we watch as the edges of the photo start to burn, setting a small fire, but there is nothing we can do. Desperately, Mary Clay tries to end the session, but it is mine, and only I can close it down – I should have pointed that out earlier.

Mary Clay screams out as her head flies back like she's been punched. She sits back in the proper position, but there is something wrong with her eyes – they are now pitch black.

"Lucy was taken because of you, Able Fredrick Wallace Junior. This is your punishment!" Her head flops to the table and she slides to the floor. Dead.

Fear grips us all, but we dare not help her. Although Mary Clay's fingers are no longer on the board, the planchette continues to move in rapid succession, spelling out "devil" over and over, until the planchette flings off the board, crashing hard against the wall – denting it. The Ovilus spits out words, unclear but very much frightening. A giggle, a scream, and growls bellow out from the device. The room starts to shake and more items crash around us.

"Who is here with us?" I scream.

Someone is running around the table, footsteps so small and fast, it has to be that of a small child. The K2 meters are spiking to red; the maximum indicator. The room is in utter chaos. The session ends so abruptly, I know there will certainly be a price to pay. In shocked disbelief, Bella is lifted off her feet and thrown hard against the wall. Matt and I rush to her knowing full well we are in trouble having broken the rules of the session, and have more than likely brought peril down upon us. Bella's arm is broken, but she is sitting up crying, alive at least. Mary Clay has slipped under the table. Her pale greying face is lined with thick black veins – the sight is horrendous. Then the room violently shakes, so we take cover in the doorway. Able Wallace is sitting at the table, frozen in terror.

Then the most diabolical scene plays out in front of us. The floor opens up, cracks apart – the noise it makes is horrifying! Inside is a gash of red, it looks like blood, it smells like rotten eggs. I gag, but hold it in. Out of the gaping hole in the floor comes a swirling black mass. It morphs and shifts, and for a split second it reveals itself. It is the Prince of the Underworld himself, Lucifer. I am petrified, as it swirls back into the black morphing mass of darkness.

"I am sorry!" Able screams at the beast. "I swear, I was going to do your work, but I got busy!"

The black mass speaks, momentarily revealing the Angel of Darkness within.

"You sold me your soul for your wealth, and the privileges you have, you owe me! I stole your daughter as a consequence of what happens when you disobey me."

It swirls around the room, reaching out towards Able, who can no longer move. A giant arm, with talons spread, grabs the terrified man and takes him back through the crack, down into the bowels of Hell.

"Mummy!" a childish voice shouts from somewhere above us.

The room returns to normal in the blink of an eye. The crack in the floor has gone, and the room has stopped shaking.

"Mummy, help me!"

Switching on all the lights as we run through the house, up the staircase, following close behind Bella, whose arm is hanging slack down the side of her body. We rush into Lucy's bedroom and are stopped dead in our tracks when we see Lucy sitting on her bed sobbing and shivering but well and truly alive. We leave the room as Bella fusses over Lucy, checking her and smothering her in kisses only a Mother can give.

Later that night, we watch and wait as an ambulance takes away the body of Mary Clay, and not long after we are ordered to check into the police station as soon as possible, or else. Together we stand by the car, looking up at the intimidating structure. Bella is holding Lucy on her lap at another ambulance who are tending to her broken arm.

Sometimes it isn't the house, nor the ghosts that haunt people, sometimes it is the deeds they do that secure their fate.

It starts to drizzle as we drive back down the driveway. In the rear-view mirror, the mansion slowly fades from view. Of course we are never going to tell anyone what happened, not even the police. I suspect they won't believe us anyway. No doubt Bella will have to come up with a plausible reason as to why her husband is now missing, and how Lucy made it home, unharmed.

"Hey, I found out my girlfriend is a ghost. I knew the minute she walked through the door."

"Shut up Ian!" Matt and I laugh.

# Problems

I am alive, but I am dead.

There was a time when I could feel, but that was eons ago.

Sometimes, I float away and disappear, but most of the time I live inside my head, not knowing what will happen from one day to the next. I don't know, when I wake, which year I will be in, nor where the Hell I'm going. That is the problem.

I would love to tell you when it started happening, but it was so very long ago that I hardly remember much of anything...That's the other problem, some of the places I end up, I have no idea where I am.

*Oh Hell, here I go again…down the tunnel of darkness…*

I'm standing in a doorway; I can't see because the room is dark. I can smell incense – Sandalwood tickles my nostrils, so I must be in my Mother's bedroom at her house, the place where I grew up. She moves in the bed and asks me to come closer. I reach out, I am just about to touch her, feel her soft hand – but it doesn't work like that. I can't actually touch anyone when I'm in transit, from one place to the next.

*Suddenly, a sparkle of colour zooms towards me…the tunnel appears and I am pulled in…*

I land hard on solid ground. It is snowing, I am looking at the sky. I don't want to be here, anywhere but here. The man with the axe is coming closer! His footsteps crunching in the snow, makes me tremor in fear. I will myself away, but it's not that simple, I can't just make it happen. I watch his approach. He is nearly in front of me. This time I can see his features. He is old, and although he looks familiar, I have no idea who he is. He is speaking; though I cannot hear his words – the wind is too loud. It's cold and I am shivering.

*I am about to scream when suddenly, I am taken away, down the tunnel…leaving the old man I do not know behind…*

I wake in my bed and the room is covered in sunshine. I feel someone next to me, and I know I have come home. Seth rolls over and touches me, he abruptly wakes in fright.

"You are back! Where have you been? You took so long this time."

It still baffles him that I live like this. I told him about my problem when we first met. That was years ago now.

"The kids have missed you," he quietly says.

"I know love, I seem to be flittering about more so now than ever. You know I can't help it. How about, I get the kids ready for school, and you can have a sleep in. Everything will be okay, the kids understand."

I leave the room and go to my children, Sophie my five-year-old daughter, and Charlie my rambunctious eight-year-old son. It has been hard for them having me leave them, sometimes in the middle of dinner, or tucking them in at night. I don't drive, because it could be dangerous if I disappear. It happened once, and I will never let that happen again.

"Charlie, wake up darling boy, I am home."

He wakes and smiles when he sees me, rubbing his tired eyes. He reaches out for me, I melt into his tiny arms, and breathe in his morning scent. A tear falls and I brush it away.

"My sweet boy, go and get ready for school, and I will meet you downstairs for breakfast. I need to wake Sophie," I pull him in tighter, I never want to let go. "I love you Charlie. You know that right?"

"Yes, Mummy. I love you too."

I go to wake Sophie. She is sitting in bed and her smile lights up some of the darkness in my soul.

"Mummy! I thought I was dreaming. I could hear you talking to Charlie. Mummy I missed you. You've been gone for days this time. I hate it when you leave."

Her tears break me. I hurry over, scooping her into my arms. For the first time in months they feel full, and real.

"Sophie, I'm sorry. I am here now, that's all that matters," I kiss her little cheeks – I smell lavender, feel her warm skin. She giggles when I tickle her tummy. "I'm going to get ready and I will see you downstairs for breakfast. Okay?"

"Okay Mummy. Promise you will stay this time?"

"Oh sweetheart, you know Mummy can't stay. But I will see how I go."

I venture back into our bedroom, joining my husband who is getting dressed for the day.

"Where did you go this time babe?" his voice croaks sullenly.

"I was with Mum for a bit. Then I ended up at that cabin in the snow, again. That man was waiting for me. He got really close this time – I was terrified."

He pats the side of the bed for me to sit down. So I do. I can feel the distance between us, a  black hole pulling us apart.

"I'm not sure how much more of this we can take. It is no good for our marriage and the kids are confused. Charlie told one of his friends about your problem, and now they think he is weird. I had to get him early from school yesterday, he is being bullied," he takes a breath to calm himself. "I know you can't help it, but you need to know, this is really affecting the kids. I'm at a loss as to what to do. I get lonely when you are away too," tears sparkle in his eyes, he brushes them away.

Although this kills me inside, and breaks my heart about the kids and the effect this is having on my husband – there is nothing I can do about it.

"Look, I have an idea. How about you take the day off work, and we keep the kids home? We could go somewhere special? We could go to the beach? They would love that," I say snuggling closer to him.

He stands abruptly and moves away.

"Really? You think that will make up for the time you spend away?"

"Seth, it is better than nothing. I would love to spend the day with you and the kids; it has been such a long time since we did anything together."

*Suddenly, my head feels funny, and there is a ringing in my ears...This is not good…I can feel the tug, like a string is pulling me towards the tunnel…Please, I beg, not now…*

I come too in complete darkness. Instantly I know where I am. The place I call The Void. I call it that because the dense dark fog is so thick it's hard to breathe, and I can hardly see two feet in front of me. I have not been here since my teenage years. The vile stench is like sewerage and off meat. Stumbling to my feet, off the cold wet ground, my clothes are drenched, they stick to me as I tread through the nothingness.

A sound to my left startles me. Something fast darks past, then another and another. Their primal noises screaming through the darkness, chills me to the core. I run.

Risking a glance back, I see a morphing cloud of black mass following me – flying and swirling around. I can feel their coldness as they pass through me – it starts at my toes and up through the top of my head. I think I will not survive this. This time, whatever they are, will rip me apart. Turning back to a fast run, I hit a tree, and I am out…

I wake and my head is swimming. It takes me a while to realise I am in the back of the old Holden we had when we first got together. Seth is driving and his brother Adrian is riding shotgun. They are talking animatedly about the movie we just watched: *Pulp Fiction*. They are laughing their heads off; Seth is stealing looks at me in the rear-view mirror.

"Did you like the movie babe?"

"Yes, I love Quentin Tarantino. He is the best," I reply.

I feel like something is missing. The kids! I have come back to before the kids were even a thought inside my head. This has never happened before. I am so confused; my head feels foggy. I don't want to be here without the kids even being in existence. I need to get away.

"Are you okay babe? You look sick."

*I don't have time to answer him, before I am dragged away…Back down the tunnel…*

When I come too, I am back at home with Mum and Dad. My older brother Emmet is eating his breakfast and packing his school bag. I sit here dumbfounded. Something strange is occurring. I keep ending up in the past.

"Sarah-Jane, eat your breakfast. Hurry up or you will miss the school bus."

I dare not move, not wanting this moment to end. Dad is alive and sitting next to me; he died several years ago from a heart attack, and I haven't seen Emmet in years – he lives overseas with his wife and children. Mum is still alive, but the times I end up in this house, she is usually in bed, existing in a deep dark depression. I take this opportunity, because I don't know if I will ever have another chance.

"Dad, I love you."

"Oh, munchkin. I love you to the moon and back."

He kisses my cheek.

"Mum, I love you too. I just want you both to know you are wonderful parents. And I am sorry if I have caused you any problems."

"Sweetheart, don't be silly. We love you too. Now go and get ready for school."

I make my way to my old bedroom. It is exactly as I had left it, all those years ago. It is messy but clean. My posters are on the walls, and the bookshelf packed with all of my favourite books. Even my stuffed animals I had forgotten I had, sit there waiting for a cuddle.

*The air in the room changes, it is charged with a new energy I have never felt before… Suddenly, I feel myself drifting towards the tunnel, but I don't want to go, not yet…But I can't stop the cycle of life that takes me away from this moment…*

The snow wakes me, and this horrifies me to no end. I am shaking, because of the cold and because of the man I know is coming. I hear his boots crunching along the snowy ground.

"You are back!" he yells.

Hearing his voice for the first time, it startles and confuses me. He comes closer and closer with his axe. Is he going to kill me?

"Who are you?" I ask, sitting up.

"You don't know who I am?" he says, clearly surprised.

"No, I don't."

"Get up, you need to come with me, before you disappear again. There are things I need to explain to you."

He helps me to my feet. I am bewildered by this sudden turn of events. Who is this man? How does he know who I am? I follow him to the cabin. His hand is wrapped firmly around the axe.

"I'd feel better if you didn't have that in your hand. What's it for anyway?"

"There are fallen trees everywhere, I can't keep up with it. I spend my days chopping the fallen ones into firewood, among other things."

I do not know him, but I believe him. We make it to the cabin. It is nice and warm inside with a fire going. He makes us both hot drinks and we sit at his little table. He keeps the place immaculate, and it smells of home. The furniture is homemade, by his hands and hard work, no doubt.

"I am your Grandpa. I thought you would have recognised me?"

"Grandpa? But you have been dead for years. I've never even met you."

"I thought you might have recognised me from photos. Besides that, you always disappear before I have the chance to talk to you. To explain things. I never see people out here. How have your adventures been?"

Lost somewhere in my thoughts, I try to dredge up the photographs in my mind of my Grandparents.

"Hold up, Dad said you were dead. Is that not true?"

"Yes, well, there are things you really need to know. I know that it is happening to you too, which is why I have tried to catch up with you whenever you come here."

So, this is why I have this problem. Did I inherit it?

"Are you saying you have the same thing? Will it ever stop? Do you still travel? I have so many questions!"

"The thing is, you will end up somewhere and you will be stuck there forever. But there are signs when this will happen. It started with me flitting around from place to place in quick succession," he takes a deep breath. I sense his burden, the same as mine. "It felt like I was being ripped apart. Then one day I came back here and I never left."

Suddenly I am scared and worry creeps through me. I wonder where I will end up if this ever ends? I pick up my hot chocolate and it tastes delicious.

*My head begins to tingle...The cup shakes in my hand, I put it down...His voice fades as I drift down the silvery tunnel...*

I'm standing next to Mum's bed. The room smells like she hasn't opened a window in months. The entire room feels damp. She is sitting up in bed smoking – a terrible habit that never abated. She looks old and withered. Pale and unwell.

I'm waiting to be pulled away, but it doesn't happen; this scares me, I quiver. Suddenly she has a coughing fit, each one worse than the other. After a while she settles. She spits into a hanky, and I see blood – she tries to hide it.

"There you are, I have been waiting," she barks at me.

Why is she acting like this? I haven't spoken to her in years. Usually I just transition through, like a train passing through a silent station. Her smoke surrounds me like a serpent. In the vapour I smell sickness and strawberries.

"Hello Mum. I think I have come to say goodbye."

She laughs and it shakes the bed.

"No, Sarah-Jane. You don't understand. This is the end of your travels. This is where you end up."

"What the fuck are you talking about?" I scream at her.

"Why do you think I stay here child?"

I do not understand. I am stunned into a swirl of confusion and deathly silence. I look around the room in deep thought, and finally the truth punches me in the gut. It wasn't Dad who I inherited this from; it was Mum all along.

Then I remember…It was Dad who took me to gymnastics, swimming lessons and parent teachers' meetings. He would flip it off by saying Mum was having a nap. Then a lost memory implodes inside my head…One day I crept into the room to see her. But she wasn't there. Nor was she in the ensuite. Her walk-in closet. Also empty. I asked Dad where she was? He lied right to my face, reassuring me she was having a nap.

Now I realise it was total bullshit! This makes me mad suddenly, all those years of lies have me fuming.

I stayed with Mum; I had no other choice. The opportunity for me to leave never eventuating. I watched her slowly wither away. No one came to the house, and we never left. Existing on nothing. We lay in her bed, me staring at the ceiling wondering what my life would have been if only I had made it back home to my husband and kids instead. I didn't want to be here, but there was nothing I could do about it. I was beginning to think I would never see my family again… After a few months, Mum died in her sleep.

Then one day I wake up back at the cabin. This time inside, not out on the snow. Grandpa is screaming in my face.

"Hurry child, we don't have much time. There is only one way you can stop bouncing around. You must kill me. This is your last chance, or you will be stuck here forever, with me. If you want to go home to your husband and kids, do as I say, do it now!"

Without a second thought, I grab the pistol from his hand. I turn it around and shoot my grandpa clear in the middle of his forehead.

*The room begins to spin, my head feels broken…The tunnel is smaller this time, and at the very end I have my bedroom in my sights. The hole in the air is closing, I run and I run...But I am exhausted, shattered beyond anything I have felt before…The colours slowly dim as I race through and lunge for the opening…*

Seth is shaking me awake.

"You are back! You came back!"

His tears soak into my dirty shirt. He smells like coconuts and after shave. Am I really here? I made it. There is a knock at the door, and the kids burst in. They pile on top of the bed and snuggle in giggling. They seem a whole head taller, and this saddens me. Something is different, I feel it in my bones. Something has settled, and there is no string attached to me anymore. I made it home and here I will stay. I hope...

# The Graveyard Shift

From the basement I take the staircase up to the ground floor. When I enter the long dark corridor, my skin is crawling. A large black creature drops down from the ceiling, exhaling death and rot into my face—it pierces me with blood red orbs, scuttles up the wall—then back along the ceiling. I blink and it's gone.

Just being here alone is making my imagination run wild. It's morgue like cold in here. A ghostly mist escapes with my breath.

The building is a massive eight storied ten-year-old apartment complex with public and residential amenities. They're called the Waterfront Apartments. There's no power at the moment, not since a fire corrupted the electrical system.

So far, I've checked through the basement where all the staff lockers, changing rooms, and cafeteria are located. A temporary office for security is situated down a long eerie concrete corridor, due to the control room being out of order – after what happened here with the shootings. I check the fitness area that takes up half of the ground floor, with a large indoor swimming pool, a sauna, and a gym, for tenants only. Basement checked off, I move along.

With the elevator out, I have to take the stairs. Up on the ground floor where it hosts a lavish restaurant, cocktail bar, and a gift shop, I rattle their doors, they're locked up tight.

Back into the chillingly dark stairwell to climb to the first floor. *Is something following me?* Startled, I point the flashlight back, and thankfully nothing is there. Though, I hear footsteps rush at me, so I hurry up the steps.

While I'm pushing open the door, a cold hand grasps my arm, making me drop the flashlight. I'm suddenly engulfed in pitch black darkness – but not before something God awful flashes before me. It's a swirling black cloud, a morphing mass sparking cobalt blue in the centre, marbled hands reach out as screams blast into my eardrums. Choosing flight, instead of freeze or fight, I scoop the flashlight off the ground, switching it on with shaking hands. In haste,

I push through the door into the hallway, and when it retracts, I jump out of my skin. I need to compose myself; I have a job to do.

The door is cold against my back as I try to catch my breath. Seconds turn into minutes, perhaps hours. I seem to have lost all concept of time. My head feels stuffed with cotton wool. I try to remember…*I entered this building at sunset.* For a minute I'm lost in the memory of the purples and magentas spreading their dawn tendrils across the sky.

I've no idea what time it is because I've accidentally left my cell phone at home in a mad dash to make it here for my shift. All the clocks I've come across have been showing different times. *Weird.* My watch has stopped at 6 am, the exact moment I entered this hell hole of a building. This place seems to be gobbling time.

Three nights ago eight people were murdered here. The police have cordoned off the areas where the shootings and the fire took place. The security firm I work for got the contract to patrol here, to ensure curious explorers and thrill seekers stay off the property. Just last night I had to run off a paranormal investigation team who begged me to let them in. They even offered me money for a tour. The boss would have had my head on a stick if I'd let them in.

The apartments have been left abandoned and the tenants are not permitted back until the investigation is through. They say it could take another two or three days. This is my second night on the graveyard shift. The police emptied the place when they got the calls about a gunman walking through the building shooting people with a rifle.

My brother Colten is a cop, and when he found out I was coming here to do security detail he called me immediately; concerned.

"Hey Gabe, how's it going?"

"Good thanks. What's up?" I asked.

"I'm wondering if you want to catch up in the weekend, have a game of basketball? I'll book us in if you want?" Colten suggested.

"Sounds good bro. How's work?" I asked.

"The murders at the Waterfront Apartments are keeping me up at night, I tell you," he exhales a huge sigh, and I can tell he is shaking his head. I know my twin brother as well as I know myself. Two peas in a pod, literally!

"Are you any closer to catching the bastard who did it?"

"No. We've not caught him yet but we know who he is. It's been a difficult investigation with all the camera footage destroyed, the evidence and whatnot, you know, after he shot the security guards."

Colten goes quiet.

"Yes, poor old Bobby Ray, he didn't deserve that, and Luke McGee has a baby on the way," I said.

"Please don't do it bro. I heard you were replacing them. I know you probably feel obligated, you and Bob were good friends. But it is dangerous there, I have heard all sorts of things about the place from other cops...really scary stuff, even some of the squad refuse to enter it now."

"Colten, you know I don't believe in that crap, ghosts and demons, goblins and ghouls, it's utter rubbish."

"Just be careful. Sometimes murderers go back to the location of the crime for the thrill and to marvel in the destruction they've caused. Look I've got to go, but I'll give you a call tomorrow. I'll see you at the B.B court at 10 am, on Saturday. Okay?"

"See you then bro. You don't need to call to check up on me. I can look after myself, always have," I said, this made us both laugh.

Chills afflict me as I recall the conversation, and goose pimples give me the jitters.

*I shake off a vision of me lying there upon the floor, dead as a doorknob, in a pool of my own blood.* I've always been told I have an overactive imagination!

I am jolted out of my reverie when I glance something big and black down the staircase. I'm in the stairwell, trying to make it to the first floor. I run up the stairs, because I can hear it following me. *It's all in my imagination*, I tell myself. Places like this give me the creeps. Not from the dead—who I don't believe in—it's the living, I fear.

Except for the light from my flashlight, the hallway is in complete darkness. It's a standard police issue torch that can be used to hammer someone in the head, I suppose.

I hear a female scream, it attacks my ears, making me drop the flashlight again. I'm all thumbs tonight. This place is freaking me out, and I seem to be chasing shadows.

In the corners the blackness is thick, deep and eternal. The scream pierces the air again, but now it is closer, almost right next to me.

I get a jolt when I hear the door at the far end of the corridor slam shut.

"Hello! Is there someone here? This place is off limits, you aren't allowed to be in here," I say trembling, but nobody responds.

A cold shiver feathers down my back. There is no way anyone could get in here; I checked all the entry and exit points as soon as I had arrived. Though now the camera screens have been destroyed there is no way for me to confirm this. I direct my light up and down the corridor as I make my way to the staircase to ascend to the second floor.

A glacial coldness touches my shoulder, making me gasp in fright. This place is playing tricks with my mind.

The second floor has a heaviness that leaves me momentarily dizzy, and I feel eyes watching me but I can't explain it. I've never had a nervous disposition but tonight my instincts are telling me to run and hide. Although the foreboding feeling is strong, I manage to check all the rooms are secured as well as the guest bathrooms.

I make it out onto the landing and start climbing towards the third floor. Last night, I couldn't get up here as the police forensic team were still investigating the crime scene. When I reach the door and open it a corpse cold blast of freezing air hits me with full force nearly knocking me over. I'm suddenly tired in my bones, finding it hard to lift my feet. I feel a heavy pressure on my chest.

I keep going…hoping to get the fuck out of here. I don't want to admit it to myself but I'm petrified.

Crime scene tape cordons off some of the corridor and a couple of the apartments. A sound somewhere behind me has me turning. I hear screams and shouts. My teeth are chattering and it's not from the cold. All of a sudden I hear gunshots blast from somewhere inside the building. That doesn't make any sense, perhaps it came from outside?

I pull the taser from my utility belt, only to be used under special circumstances, and this is one of those moments. It's the only thing I have to protect myself. Normally, I'd be armed but since the building is empty the bosses deemed it unnecessary to carry. Unaware of where the noises, gunshots, and screams are coming from, I walk deeper into the bowels of the building. Stepping over the yellow and black tape, I hear gunfire again. This time I duck for cover.

I know in my soul this is all wrong. Whatever is happening, I can't make sense of. The shots blast all around me hitting nothing. I run for my life along the hallway. A huge black shadow darts towards me, I feel it pass through my body, knocking the wind from me. Although I'm beyond scared, and operating on adrenaline in autopilot mode, I carry on, I need to get this done.

I check that all the apartment doors on this floor are locked up and secure, the guest bathrooms too. Though admittedly, it is getting challenging to ignore all the noises coming from every direction. I need normal noise, so I start humming to myself. But that doesn't last long, when I hear a loud crashing sound thundering along the corridor, it's brutally loud that I have to cover my ears. I search the hallway and discover all the doors are wide open! I know they were closed only moments ago.

"What the fuck?" I yell.

Suddenly, a thought invades my mind. The murderer could still be here, like Colten had warned. A vision of the madman bursts inside my head...*Him killing his girlfriend, and then his mother, then shooting two kids and their parents on the fourth floor* – only a sick and evil person can do something like that.

I hear giggling behind me. I'm stopped dead in my tracks when I spot two small shadows dart past in my peripheral. It chills me to the core. I walk faster along the corridor and come to the spot where Bobby was killed. I'm saddened when I see his blood dried stiff to the carpet. I'm shoved hard in the back making me fall to my knees. *Perhaps I just tripped on something?*

My adrenalin is spiking through the roof. More gunshots have me off the ground; bolting up the stairs to the fourth floor. It is dark and eerie, and excessively cold. As the door shuts me in I feel hands all over my body but there is no one there! I move away from the door and make my way towards the second crime scene. I'm really not supposed to be on this floor but I need to check I am actually alone. The pressure is back on my chest. Then I feel hands around my throat. I'm trying to catch my breath, when it tightens its hold around my neck. My scream reverberates down the corridor when I am released. I fall to the floor in a heap and I don't have the strength to get up. Pure fear grips me hard.

I want to be home, watching a ball game with Roxie, my BullDog sitting next to me, drinking a beer, and having a laugh with my buddies. If only they could see me now, the sceptic, running from shadows and things that frankly do not exist. I can see them cracking up at my foolishness. But they aren't here: I'm by myself.

I thought I could do this, but it is getting nearly impossible to compose myself.

I drag my body off the floor, inhaling deep breaths to calm my nerves. I am in full throttle terror. I can't remember arriving here. Something inside my head feels broken. I recall driving here in my Ute, I can visualise the last thing I saw before I entered; the sun rising.

There is a scuttling sound coming towards me; I hear its claws scratching on the walls. Pointing my light towards the sound, I see it, it's horrid and ghastly. It's clinging to the ceiling upside down, it's arms, exponentially long that they nearly touch me. As quick as humanly possible I hoof it down the corridor to the other end of the floor. I make my way to the other staircase. I want out. I quit. I'm done. I have never been more scared in my entire life. What I just saw confirms to me that I shouldn't be here.

Although I am confused and my memory is unreliable at the moment, I do recall what Bobby had said about this building the last time we spoke a couple of weeks ago. It was his two-year anniversary working here, and I said I was happy for him. But then he mentioned some bizarre information. He was seeing a counsellor about the things that had been happening in his life. His world was falling apart.

I'd tried to remind him that he has a loving wife and three children who depend on him. He'd said that the job was starting to mess with him and he was certain he was being haunted by spirits in the building, he'd seen things in the corner of his eyes, shadows seem to be following him everywhere. He was scared. Not just at work but they seem to have followed him home. I laughed at him, saying he obviously needed a holiday. Guilt rips a hole in my heart as I remember my blatant lack of sympathy.

When I make it back to the office I am shaking and sweating all over, and cold chills attack me. I stuff my gear into my backpack getting ready to leave the building. When suddenly three knocks pound on the office door, frightening me. It's so loud against the silence of the room. Though, it could be someone coming to replace me from the graveyard shift.

Or the police could be here to resume their investigation. When I open the office door there is a man standing there with a rifle pointed at me. I gasp in a startled breath. Time slows down as I wait for the inevitable click of the trigger. When it happens I am not surprised. I look him deep into his eyes, and they are soulless, black and empty. His smile is lopsided as the trigger releases, the pain hits me an instant later.

I come to and the man has vanished. I check myself over to be sure – I appear to be okay. I stand, stumble my way up the staircase to the front doors. Desperately, I try to get out, but the key I used to get in, it doesn't work! What the hell is going on? I start running when I hear more gunshots pursuing me. I rush to the other exits but I can't escape the building. I look back and see the hole in my stomach as I lay in a pool of blood.

I am distressed. Now I will never see my brother Colten again; I should have listened to him. Our parents will be distraught, and I don't think they will be able to handle this.

Dying is not what I'd expected. No cracking open of heaven, the earth still spins. The world doesn't stop, it keeps rotating.

Lost in the memory of what happened, a vision grips me right before I'm taken under. I see what actually happened. In my mind it plays out like a horror movie, over and over repeating itself, until I grasp the reality of it all. I am dead. So, I stop running. There is a tunnel and I decide to follow the light. I see Bobby Ray, and he tells me to go back. I ask back where? And I wake in the hospital attached to monitors.

Relief floods me. Colten's hand is warm in mine, and our parents are sitting either side of me.

I am alive! I survived the graveyard shift from hell

# An Earthly Experience

I hear the humans say I'm in a coma. That is only partly true...this human vessel I've entered is lying on a bed, hooked up to beeping machines and devices I do not recognise. Fear grips me and I don't want to be here. I need to return to my planet, Zoron. I fell into this world they call Earth, purely by accident.

We were heading to another galaxy, on a mission to rescue one of our planets from an encroaching battle – when suddenly we took an unexpected turn, a disruption in the system sending us spiralling and pitching.

We ended up diverting through the Milky Way's Asteroid Belt, crashing into Earth's atmosphere, obliterating the craft. When finally, I landed, my essence was absorbed by this vessel I am now in. For our voyages, we leave our bodies attached to an apparatus called a Simpod, so only our essence travels, making it easier to pass through other realms, dimensions and planetary systems. Something unusual is going on inside this body, I can't explain. I assess it has something to do with human emotions. Zoronians don't feel emotions, so I recognize these are coming from somewhere deep within this human being.

Some type of liquid sporadically drips from its eyes. Around me I hear the humans communicating…their voices and their language are very strange to me.

"Doctor, his heartbeat is regular, and I've also seen some tears. Other than that there still hasn't been any movement. Have the police found out who he is yet?"

"No, they are looking into missing persons cases, thus far they haven't got back to me."

"Do you think he will wake soon?"

"Hmmm…It's hard to say, his vitals are good, his brain seems to be functioning. Give it a bit more time. I'll go and check if the police have returned my call."

I hear a door close, it's loud. Sensing finally I am alone, we open our eyes, but close them tight again because the light is too bright – it hurts this body. *Pain;* I've heard the humans communicating about it. I have gathered by their words, that pain is something humans feel. Hurt and pain are bad for this species, but it is necessary for them; this is how they distinguish if there is something wrong with them. Zoronians don't feel pain or hurt, so this is an enigma about humans that we do not comprehend.

When one of them said they were about to prick me with something sharp, to see if I could feel this *pain* they are talking about, they said I felt nothing. Nothing: is another concept I do not understand. Pain can be something, or it can be nothing. Pain is hurt…very strange indeed.

When finally my eyes adjust to the light, I can see functionally. I assess the environment. The light I thought was a source inside this little box they call a room, is actually coming through some sort of shield to the outside world – it must be their sun. We learned about this planet Earth, back home on Zoron. They teach us about other galaxies and planetary systems, for knowledge and to gain vital information. Earth is on a lower echelon, and it is one of many recycling planets. When humans die, their energy or spirit is born into another vessel; they call it reincarnation, we call it recycling.

Due to humans being unaware, distracted – they will never know this about themselves, nor their real purpose for existing.

Humans believe they are alone in the Universe, and that other species like ours don't exist. Though they are getting very close to discovering the truth, they never will.

Unless we are ordered to save this planet from total annihilation, we will not venture here. Though we are not under any obligation to intervene, when the moment comes, and humans need our help, a decision will be made by the Universal Councils.

Humans have weapons that can destroy themselves instantaneously. Much the same way other recycling planets have perished, due to their inability to work out their internal conflicts.

Travellers have been ordered to stay away from Earth; it is strictly prohibited. If humans were to realise our existence on this planet, they would imprison and experiment on us. Worse than that, they could find a way to use our travel crafts and our technology, giving them the ability to cross over into other realms.

If that were to happen, it would be a disaster, they could destroy our planet. We know that humans are capable of creating, but they also have the destruction gene to destroy. I want to go home, back to Zoron. There is too much noise here. Fortunately, I am able to understand the human language, most probably because of the vessel I'm immersed in.

The humans return to the room, and I close my eyes again.

"...yes we are certain it is him, doctor. His name is James Hill. He's been missing for one week, and his wife is on her way to see him."

"Super. That ends that mystery. Good news all around. His brain waves suggest he might wake any moment, but definitely within a day or two.

Then you can take a statement from him. But as you can see, he is in no fit condition to answer any questions just yet."

"Of course, Doctor White. I understand. The wife, Maddison Hill, she's been frantic with worry. When he didn't return from his early morning run, she called it in and filed a missing person's report. As you already know, the first seventy-two hours are the most vital stages to finding a missing person, any time after that is like searching for the proverbial needle in the haystack. It's very fortunate they found him when they did."

"Yes, he was quite a mess when they brought him in. Someone found him near death in the scrub around a golf course. But the good news is he didn't suffer any long-term effects from the hypothermia, other than this temporary coma; he was unconscious when the paramedics brought him in."

*I* wasn't in a coma – James was. The impact from me colliding into him, affected his body to where we were only able to crawl into the bush, hidden amongst the trees. We lay out there in the cold. I could sense his vessel was dying...

*Would I die a human death too? What would happen to my essence if this vessel were to die – would I be stuck here for an eternity, waiting to be saved?* My mind is a racing mess; my thoughts, scrambled.

James is waking slowly inside his mind; I hear his thoughts; he is trying to comprehend what has happened. They say his wife is on her way in. I don't know what to do. I'll have to wait and see if the Zoronians come for me. Our eyes are heavy...James drifts off to sleep. His body is still unwell.

"You found him! Where was he? My God, this is amazing, I thought that something terrible had happened to James when he didn't return from his run. He didn't take any identification with him, and he'd left his cell phone at home."

We are startled awake by a loud voice. Our eyes spring open without *my* consent. James is responding to his wife's voice. I feel the touch of her skin, and it shoots shockwaves through us I cannot explain. It's almost like the way us Zoronians communicate. We have a sacred symbol called a Zoroglyph above our eyes that we use to greet one another. By merely touching each other's Glyphs, we are able to communicate our thoughts, ideas, and personal information. With our eyes fully open, their lips touch; it momentarily stops our breath! I've never felt anything like it. The liquid that was falling from our eyes before, is flooding down the side of our face.

"This is brilliant progress! He's responding to you, and look you woke him up, like sleeping beauty, you certainly have a strong bond. We'll keep him in for a couple of days to assess and monitor him. Then you can take him home, I bet your kids will be excited to see him?"

"We have all missed him dreadfully! We've been beside ourselves with worry."

A few days later, and now we are traveling in a vehicle slower than I am used to. This is a strange concept. On Zoron, our vehicles fly, and don't travel so low to the ground. Apparently, we are heading home to the family.

I have assessed that home is the place they live in, and family is James's wife and children? Maddison is driving, we pass huge buildings, houses where humans live, and other unrecognisable structures.

There are long vehicles called trains – Maddison mentions that James rides it to go to work, and that a storm damaged some of the tracks.

Back home, we learned about this perception of work humans do, to make money to survive, because they need to eat. The source, the one who made Earth, gave humans that desire inside them.

It is what gets them to do the things they do; it keeps them productive. If they didn't have this pre-programmed into them, they would die off. Which of course is inevitable, with recycling planets. One day, their sun will be their ending.

Each planet has been programmed for one thing or another. On Zoron, we are programmed to protect, defend and rescue.

Due to the fact humans are lower beings, their consciousness hasn't adapted, developed or enlightened to their higher selves. They use only a small percentage of their brain capacity, and they will never reach full comprehension, until the fifth-dimension merges with their third. The idea that their fourth dimension is in the centre of their Earth, will not be realised until the dimensions are all merged to where they should be.

It's the dimension only a few enlightened humans have ever reached. There are creatures there that were once banished from Earth; they made the fourth dimension to save themselves from extinction.

Finally, the vehicle stops at the house they call a home; we follow Maddison inside. I hear something loud to our ears, it shocks me, but it propels James forward. I cover our ears from the overwhelming shrieks and screams.

I can sense Maddison looking at us strangely, so I remove our hands from our ears. When we enter a room, two children come running and it scares me. We back away. There are no children on Zoron, we have no need for these beings. Something is happening inside us, I feel this surge of warmth, it's a comforting feeling when they wrap themselves around our legs. James scoops them up and holds them to us; warm, salty, liquid streams from our eyes.

James seems to have taken over, which is good and unexpected. I can sense our mergence into one another is getting stronger the longer I am in James's body. I am becoming James, but I am also Orwinozon.

We are named after the place we are from; Zoron. Part of my name is in honour of our God, Zorwin, who rules over our galaxy.

Back home I am what humans call a doctor. I use magic and technology to ensure all Zoronians are operating properly. We have capsule mods that can sense any problems, and the machine fixes the defects.

For hours we do human things. We eat, which is new to me. On Zoron we don't need food to sustain us, we have no need for it in our physiology. But James needs food. We help to bathe the children, and their giggles make the edges of our mouth turn up towards our eyes. There is a feeling attached to this action that makes James happy…a building pressure inside our head, I sense it might burst, but it doesn't – so I gather that the opposite of pain is happiness?

The rush of feelings leaves me momentarily stunned; humans are a complicated race. They have feelings that make them react…this is a result of their source giving them the freedom of choice.

Eventually, we enter a room, towards a bed. James takes over again and makes it right. We can feel Maddison's skin against us, and it makes us tingle and swell. I can't settle, so we lay here allowing James's thoughts to process what is happening to him, at the same time, my mind is seeking a way that I can return home. I wonder when my crew are coming to get me. I know they will be searching for me; they need me. I ponder the differences between our species. We have bodies too, but not like humans. Zoronians are much larger and there are no differences within our species, we don't have individual personalities like humans do.

We are all the same: equal. We do not die, because there is no concept of time.

Maddison cuddles into us, and we wrap her in our arms – making James feel safe. When she starts kissing us, we are overloaded and something inside our body wants to burst apart. Gently we push her away.

"What happened to you my love? Please tell me, I need to know. You've been avoiding the elephant in the room. You seem different. Almost distant..."

"I was jogging in the park that backs onto the golf course. I don't remember much. I was struck by something, maybe a falling tree? I woke up in the hospital when I heard your voice, like you were pulling me out of a trance."

She whispers, "I love you. I was so worried, I hardly slept. Will you just hold me while we fall asleep? I'm so tired – the stress has been affecting me."

"I'm sorry," is all I can manage to say as our eyes close.

The night is dark and thick. The Earth's moon is up in the sky, full and white. I couldn't sleep, so we had to get up. We wander around the house in the dark, because I can see well without the light. I feel lost. James feels lost.

I am stuck inside someone else's body, and although James is trying to close his eyes, from exhaustion, I can't stop the thoughts pushing through my mind.

My planet Zoron is beautiful. Although Earth has some good things going for it, it is a dreadful place, there is too much chaos and noise.

On Zoron, we have many moons and many suns. The land is not hilly and rough like Earth, there are no build-up of structures. There are no natural formations, like rivers or oceans, forests or farms, and animals are native to Earth. Everything on Zoron is regimental.

We are given a task to do, and it stays that way for an eternity. We live in towers that reach the sky. There is no internal war, like humans have, with their weapons, destruction and devastation towards one another. We all get along because we have one purpose, and that is to function as a member of the Zoronians, in a way that ensures our survival against other planets from other galaxies.

If we didn't all work together, we would fall into the grasps of another galactic force. We are the colour of everything around us. We change to adapt to our surroundings. We blend in. In our essence state we are invisible.

We are in the room they call the kitchen, the place they make food, when suddenly there are bright lights beaming into the room. I don't know what is happening. Suddenly, we hear a voice inside our head…saying in my language, *to come outside*. So we do.

When we venture out, a beam of light hits us and we fall down. The grass is cold and wet beneath us, it is an unpleasant feeling. The voice is commanding I enter the travel craft, so I detach myself from James and as I am pulled into the air, into the craft, I watch as Maddison runs out of the house, she leans over James who is still lying on the ground. She freezes when she sees the craft; her eyes are wide and her mouth agape.

James sits up as we fly away; looking dazed. I am surrounded by my crew, though one is missing. Perhaps they didn't survive the crash into Earth? Well I certainly have a story to tell the others when I get home.

We zoom through the sky and up into space towards the wormhole we were supposed to have gone through initially. Earth disappears from my view, and although I hated the place,

I have learned so much more than they ever taught us. Although, the human race fight and many are lost, they have something we have no concept of: love. They love as much as they destroy. I could feel that love, and I will miss it, even though I only felt it for a moment, it will stay with me forever.

# Broken in the Dark

A group of five teenagers and two adults are trekking through an eerily thick forest; their destination, Sunnyvale Camping Grounds, in the Coromandel, New Zealand.

Sunrays filter through gaps in the ancient mammoth trees, casting an ominous dark shadow upon the forest floor.

Greg Hamilton is a new instructor to the group, he'll be taking over from the camp leader Carol Hughs when she retires after this; her last trek taking kids into the bush to teach them confidence and survival skills. Her body is weary, bones aching; twenty-five years of doing this is taking a toll on her body. As she walks, her mind is drifting away on a cruise ship in the Caribbean with her husband Troy, lapping up the sun while drinking cocktails next to the pool.

Just three more days until freedom.

They've prepared to lose cell phone signal the deeper into the woods they travel, so Carol is entrusting Greg to negotiate the map. The trail inclines as they near a ridge, which Greg believes will take them directly to the camping grounds. However, at the top he shouts for Carol to join him.

The campground is not at the bottom of the gully, like he had thought, only more hills raise their heads into the pale cerulean sky.

"What's up?" Carol pauses, pursing her lips, looking around, shaking her head. "Where is the compass?" she asks, holding out her hand.

"I thought you had it," Greg responds; perplexed.

The teens sit on the rocks munching on energy bars, while the facilitators appraise the map intently. Carol decides they need to forge ahead. If they keep on this path they should intercept another trail that will direct them to the campgrounds. She'd been so busy inside her head, planning and dreaming, that she'd become complacent.

The group walk on, the kids chattering amongst themselves, Carol downtrodden, and Greg disheartened for not paying closer attention to their location – he can't fathom how he managed to get them lost.

When they reach the point they should be crossing with the other trail, Carol is appalled to see it no longer exists. It's all gorse and dense impenetrable bush. Fury grabs her in a panic, she snatches the map from Greg, accidentally ripping it in half. Everyone pauses, the teens look on, engrossed by the adults' hostility.

Carol storms off to calm herself.

By the time she returns, the sun is kissing the horizon, and the sky ablaze in twilight pinks and golds.

"I've found somewhere we can camp for the night, but we need to leave now, it's going to take us a while to get there, and it looks like rain is coming," Carol informs the team.

Black clouds amass above them as they traverse the rough terrain. The raindrops fall like little pebbles; hard, cold, and annoying. She can't understand the weather change. The forecast for the week was for sunshine and clear summer skies.

When finally they enter the clearing Carol's found, the temperature suddenly plummets, making her shiver – the sun deserted this area hours ago. Darkness crawls across the heavens.

Charlotte and Damian are instructed to gather firewood, as the camp is set up against a rock face, the fire should be able to withstand most of the deteriorating weather. The rest of the group erect four of the pop-up tents; Carol deciding it will save time and resources if they doubled-up. Greg lights a fire, bathing them is some warmth.

Later that night, Matt and Andy are sharing a tent. The incessant DRIP, DRIP, DRIP, of the rain stealing any chance of sleep. Darkness smothers them, a cold chill nestles into their bones, and although they are snuggled tight within their sleeping bags, warmth is a distant memory. A brutally loud crunching sound outside the tent snaps them awake. In the distance they hear a chilling scream. Both reach for their flashlights gripped in terror, the light illuminating them in a ghoulish way. The tent shakes on all sides, nearly buckling in the middle.

"Cut it out guys!" Matt yells, thinking it is the others playing a prank.

As lightning strikes burst like fireworks in the sky, Andy pokes his head out through the zipper, and when he sees that all of the other tents have disappeared, he's mortified! Thunder roars above them as they clamber out of the tent. Bewildered and scared, they run around trying to find everyone. Nothing makes sense. *Where did everybody go?* A horrendous snapping sound of branches, something big is moving, coming closer…they try to run but are knocked down by gigantic boulders smashing through the trees. Both are pummelled into a ghastly mash of human soup.

Meanwhile in another tent, Damian is sleeping. Greg yawns and stretches and is about to roll over into a more comfortable position, when he hears a loud crashing sound that nearly makes him jump out of his skin.

"Did you hear that?" he asks Damian, but receives nothing but soft snores in response.

Greg can't sleep because his bladder needs relieving. He climbs out of the tent, closes the zipper, and roams over to the nearest tree. He's doing his thing when suddenly he is startled by a bright blue light flashing through the woods. When he finishes, he decides to investigate; perhaps one of the kids is out there lost. The light keeps moving, and Greg follows. Unaware of his surroundings, he drops through an old abandoned mineshaft that shutdown over a hundred years ago.

As he falls into the abyss, his body turns and twists, a pitiful scream escapes his mouth, which is swiftly swallowed by the mineshaft.

Damian has waited long enough; he was terrified when he woke to find himself alone. His flashlight emits a weak yellow glow, and he has to hit it a couple of times to get it to work properly. He is blasted by cold sleet when he opens the zipper.

"Greg, are you out there?" he calls, the wind whips away his words.

He crawls out into the night. The ground is drenched, sloshing through the mud in bare feet with his flashlight spreading over the campsite, he is devastated to find all of the tents are gone. Damian is abruptly and viciously lifted off the ground, upside down into a tree, dragged right to the very top as cold wet wings wrap themselves around him.

When knife sharp claws release him, his neck snaps when body meets ground, a bloody crumpled mess at the bottom of an ancient tree.

Charlotte and Serena are restlessly sleeping, when Carol bursts into the tent, frightening them both awake.

"Get up, we need to go," she yells as she pulls at their sleeping bags, to get them up and out.

"Why? What's wrong?" Charlotte is scared seeing the horror in Carol's eyes.

They hear it through the storm; something is splitting the forest apart. The trees shake and bend in ludicrous ways. Carol hastily scans the campsite, waiting for the girls, who emerge hesitantly from their tent.

They're nearly out and free, when a huge tree falls right across them, mashing the girls into a pulpy glob of bones and bloody matter. Carol throws up – expunging herself from the harrowing sight. The girls can't be saved, so she runs for her life.

Moments before her flashlight dies for good, she spots an entrance to a cave, and makes her way inside. Huddled behind a rock, close to the entrance, she can see something black  and huge, cast in distant lightning strikes, drawing closer. Seconds later, a rod of lightning hits a tree just outside the cave, it exposes something truly atrocious; Carol can't find her voice to scream. It's a ginormous black creature standing at least ten feet tall, with red glowing eyes. It wrenches her off the ground by her hair. Its face is monstrous, disfigured, and the putrid and vile stench coming from its mouth makes her vomit.

Sharp deadly claws dig into her soft flesh, before it dumps her on the ground, knocking her out when her head greets rock.

Carol wakes on cold hard dirt as the sun peeps into the cave; dispersing some of the shadows. Pain consumes her. When she touches her head and her fingers come away bloody, she nearly faints.

She departs the relative safety of the cave, aimlessly walking, despondent and concussed. She has no idea where she is going, and can't remember where she has been. Though Carol does recall smashing her head on the ground. Perhaps the knock to her head has erased some of her memory, because she can't make sense of what happened.

Her energy levels are practically depleted, and her fear is total, but she has to get to safety; knowing that being out in the forest without equipment will be dangerous, and if hypothermia sets in it could be fatal. Her mind is a ruminating mess of thoughts and images. If only she can find the strength to make it to town, gather the right people to come out to search for the others.

Eventually, she stumbles onto tarmac, as day turns to night. Trudging along the lone wet slippery road, all she wants to do is sleep.

Worn, battered, and bloodied, she finally reaches the police station.

They place her in a warm room that has a soft couch, she sits down and immediately sleep wants to drag her under. She's given a hot chocolate to warm her insides. A detective enters the room not long after, he inhales in a deep breath, ending in a long trembling sigh, as he sits upon one of the plastic chairs.

As a doctor tends to her wounds, the detective places a dusty and worn manilla folder on the table. On the front it says, MISSING: 2010. He hands it over to Carol, who flips it open. All of the teens, as well as hers and Greg's names, are attached to a photograph, the one they took right before they entered the forest. Seeing their bright eager faces all lit up in the sunshine, it fills her heart with dread. They look so happy, and now they are all missing or could be dead.

"Where did you find this?" she asks the sullen looking detective.

"Well, when the kids didn't return home, their parents contacted us and reported them missing. Your husband had been going frantic, I remember that – it almost broke my heart. One of the searchers found what we believe to be Greg Hamilton's Nikon digital camera. We had the photos developed, this is the only photo on it."

Carol's face darkens as her eyes gaze into the distance, trying her hardest to remember. Something about all of this doesn't feel right; it niggles in the back of her mind.

"Have you found the others?" she asks, her hope rising.

"No, we have not found any of them," he matter-of-factly responds.

"How long have I been missing?"

"That's something we need to talk to you about," replies the detective.

The doctor leaves them alone, gently closing the door behind him.

"How long detective?" Carol pushes him on.

"How about you answer some questions before you get to ask yours, okay?"

"Okay, fair enough."

"So let's start with, how long do you think you have been missing?"

"No longer than two days, give or take. As you can see I have a gash on my head, so I think my perception of time may be a little muddled."

"Where are the rest of your group?" He sits up straighter in the chair, leaning towards her eagerly.

"I remember seeing the girls, Charlotte and Serena. But I have no idea where any of the others are. I didn't see them after we all went to sleep. I wish I could tell you more, but I don't know anything that could help," she says as the tears roll down her cheeks.

"How did you sustain the head injury?"

She touches the bandage. "I think I slipped somewhere on my way back through the forest." She wipes away the tears with her sleeve.

"Why all the questions, detective?"

"You went missing in 2010," he states, pursing his lips tightly.

"So what! You've already told me that." Her anger rises along with her fear.

"What year is it Mrs Hughs?"

"Carol, just call me Carol please."

"Okay then, Carol, what year is it?"

"It's December, 2010. Why do I feel like you are playing games with me?"

"Sorry, but I just needed to know when you last saw the rest of your team. It's due process in an incident like this." He continues. "It's the year 2023. You have been missing for thirteen years."

Carol can't talk, she feels her heart racing at the facts he is relaying to her. She frets, wondering where the hell she has been for the last thirteen years.

The detective informs her that her husband is on his way in. She sits and waits. All the while, her memory returns in shattered pieces, and in a broken mess she crumples to the floor on her knees and sobs – as she remembers it all. Carol knows she will have to explain everything that happened, especially to the parents of the lost children. Her mind drifts to the creature in the cave, and although she'd love to tell the detective about it, she knows he'll think she's gone mad in the head, or worse, that she did something terrible to the teens and Greg – so she remains silent. For the rest of her living days, she never tells a soul about what really happened in the forest that day. She knows they won't believe her.

# The Gilded Mirror

It's a beautiful sunny afternoon, until we enter the antique store. An icy cold settles around us as the door seals us in. Outside the front windows, the sky darkens as a black ominous cloud unexpectedly hides the sun away. It unsettles me for some reason. The store smells of old people, mothballs, and musky furniture.

It's a relatively smaller building compared to the other two antique stores we've just perused. After about ten minutes of searching, I spot the item I want – a gilded mirror for our bedroom.

"What about this one?" I ask my husband Cody.

"Yeah, but it looks pricey," he remarks.

I look at the price tag and I'm surprised to see it's only a hundred and fifty dollars.

It's faded a little with age, but it still retains the gold trim around the border. It has claw feet at the base, and it's leaning up against a dresser drawer, since it's probably too heavy to mount onto a wall. There are intricate inscriptions of flowers and leaves running up and down the sides. At the very top is a symbol, a cross inside a star, in the centre of a crown.

We approach the elderly man behind the counter, who's busy punching buttons on an ancient looking calculating machine.

"Hello. Sorry to disturb you, but I want to inquire about the gilded mirror."

"What about it?" he grumps.

"I'm just wondering if I've read the price tag correctly?"

He looks me up and down with a toothy grin, giving me the creeps for some reason.

"Oh, that one. You read it right. I dropped the price because it's not selling for some reason."

"Okay. I think it'd be perfect for our bedroom," I remark.

"Would you take a hundred for it?" Cody asks.

"Hmmm...make it a hundred and twenty-five," the owner barters.

"How about, since it's not selling, we'll take it off your hands for a hundred and fifteen?" Cody smiles.

"Deal," says the old man. "It's a real bargain. It's very old and heavy so you'll need both of you to carry it, since my trolley is busted, and I have a sore back."

Cody chimes in. "I'll swing the car around the back, and we'll lay it down on the backseat."

As we're driving home with Cody at the steering wheel, I can't stop peering back at the mirror. Something about it pleases me; whether it's due to the fact it's an old relic from another era, or because I usually become a bit obsessed whenever I purchase new items for the house.

A week later, I'm in our bedroom upstairs readying myself for our dinner date. It's 5pm. I'm kneeling on the floor in front of the mirror using the hair straightener, when I hear tapping coming from somewhere inside the room. I lean in close to the mirror, and sure enough it's coming from there.

I look behind it, in case it's a rodent, however, there's nothing there to explain the sounds. I scamper down to Cody, and I find him in the kitchen pouring himself a glass of merlot.

"Whoa, what's up?" he asks as I nearly collide into him. "You look like you've seen a ghost."

"It's nothing," I say, omitting the truth. "I'm just wondering how much longer you're going to be. Our reservation is at six o'clock, and I don't want to be late," I say, distracting him.

When we arrive home a couple of hours later, we discover the house in a shambles. The couches in the living room have shifted from their usual spot, a lazy-boy chair is tipped over, and books from the shelving unit lay discarded upon the floor. The kitchen is in worse shape. The cold-water tap is on full blast, and since there are dishes in the sink, it's flooded the room.

We decide against calling the police, since nothing is missing or broken. With everything back in its rightful place, we dry the floor with towels.

I'm in bed reading, and Cody is finishing off paperwork in his home office. Suddenly, I hear the tapping sound again, but this time it's much louder, more like a slight knocking. I switch off the bedside lamp, and snuggle in bed, ignoring it.

I'm woken by the sound of voices in the room, but I know I must be dreaming, so I drift back to sleep. I toss and turn the rest of the night.

When I wake in the morning, Cody's in the shower. I have chores to catch up on, so I dress and make my way to the kitchen. I switch on the kettle. While I'm pouring cereal into a bowl, I hear a horrendous crash above me. Thinking that perhaps Cody's fallen over, I race up the staircase.

I'm horrified to discover all of our picture frames in the hallway are shattered to pieces on the floor.

"What the fuck?"

I'm frozen in place. Cody races out of our bedroom.

"What happened?" he asks.

"I don't know! I found it this way."

It takes a while to clean up the mess. After binning the bits of glass and damaged frames, we sit down to have coffee and to contemplate.

"It must have been an earthquake," Cody's hypothesising. "But that doesn't make sense because other items would have fallen over too."

I just nod; lost in my own thoughts. My coffee is cold. I'm shaking but I don't know what is unsettling me. I've a bad feeling churning away inside my gut.

"Anyway, I'd better get ready for tonight," he says, kissing my cheek before he walks away.

Evening slowly brings an amber glow into the house.

"Right, I'm off," Cody says in high spirits.

He grabs the keys off the hook beside the front door. His friend is having a stag party, and because Cody isn't a big drinker, they've appointed him as the designated sober driver for the night.

Midnight approaches. I'm sitting in the living room watching a trashy television show. Exhaustion makes me yawn. It's stormy outside, and the wind batters the windows. The lights start flickering in the room. *It must be the storm.* I hear the front door open and close. I'm waiting for Cody to come into the room to tell me about his night, but he doesn't appear.

Curious, I walk over to the window, but the car isn't in the driveway. *Strange!* I'm certain I heard him arriving home. I've just settled back on the couch, when all of a sudden, a loud thump on the floor above has me instantly on high alert. It must be coming from our bedroom. I uncurl myself from the seat, so I can go upstairs to investigate.

As I ascend the staircase, I hear footsteps rushing behind me. I hurry into our bedroom and lock the door. I'm so scared I'm trembling. *Has someone broken into the house?* I didn't see anyone come up the stairs, although I could clearly hear footsteps chasing me. Then three loud knocks pound on the bedroom door.

I jump onto the bed freaking out. In my haste to check out the noise, I've left my cell phone downstairs, and we don't have a landline phone, or I'd call Cody. Three loud knocks in the closet have me hiding behind the armchair in the corner of the room. The knocking continues, this time on the closed ensuite door.

Slowly I rise to leave the room. I've had enough. When I pass by the mirror, I'm stopped dead in my tracks. There are people gathering inside the mirror. At first, they appear as black shadowy figures. I can't peel my eyes away from the scene. I'm beyond confused by what I'm seeing, as they morph into people cloaked in black. I touch the glass gently, and it feels like water. I reach my hand through, but instantly pull it back in horror. I'm propelled forward, I can't stop myself. I walk right into the mirror.

I wake, and I'm outside on the front lawn, as the rain hits my face. I sit up dazed and bewildered. I run inside and lock the door. Backed up against it, dripping water onto the floor, I try to catch my breath. I grab my cell phone from the living room. I'm about to call Cody, but I decide against it – not wanting to ruin his night. I wait in the living room, and eventually I must have fallen asleep, because sometime later Cody is shaking me awake.

"Babe. You're soaking wet!" he remarks, as he pulls me to my feet. "What happened to you?"

I can't reply because my teeth are chattering. He turns on the shower. The warm water disperses some of the biting cold.

Later, we're in bed and I can't stop ruminating. *How did I end up outside?* I know I should tell Cody what happened, but he'll think I'm crazy.

Things settle down for a few days. Nothing weird transpires.

However, four days later, we're sitting at the table eating dinner, when out of nowhere, all the cupboards in the kitchen fly open of their own volition. Tins of food, glassware, and crockery become airborne, they hover in mid-air, before crashing to the ground. Cody gets up to examine the mess, when he's violently knocked flat onto his backside by an invisible force. I rush over and help him off the floor.

"What the hell? What's happening?" he barks.

He looks terrified; his eyes are the size of plates.

"I don't know!" I cry. "This has been going on ever since we brought that darn mirror. I think we need to get rid of it," I say with tears welling in my eyes.

I'm overwhelmed about Cody being knocked over. It's getting out of hand.

"What are you talking about? What things?" he blurts.

"It doesn't matter, let's just forget about it for now. I'll ring the antique place in the morning and talk to the owner. He might have an explanation," I say as a cold chill passes through me, like someone just walked over my grave.

We decide to hunker down in the living room on the fold out bed because I don't want to be in our bedroom after everything that's been going on.

"I think you're withholding information from me," Cody states as his face heats in anger.

I've never seen Cody act this way before – it's very disturbing.

"Look, I'm sure there is nothing to worry about," I say, trying to placate him.

The next day and while Cody's in town, I call the antique store. I'm perplexed when a recording says the number is inactive and to check I've dialed correctly. Perhaps there's a problem with the connection? I decide that when Cody gets back, I'll pop over to the store.

He returns home, not long after. I drive into town. Although I would have liked Cody to accompany me, he has work to do, and I didn't want to bother him with this bizarre situation.

It's a twenty-minute drive to the store. However, when I make it there, it's completely abandoned. There's a grate covering the door, and when I gaze in through the windows, the place is empty. In fact, it looks like it's been closed for years. This makes no sense. An unnerving feeling pervades me as I walk back to the car. I can't shake the unease gripping me. Though the afternoon sun warms my face as I drive, it doesn't lift my mood. Aggressively I slam on the brakes, because in the rear-view mirror I can see someone is sitting on the backseat. Slowly I turn my head to look, but there's nobody there. I race home a mortified mess.

As twilight descends, I'm making dinner, when Cody rushes in through the front door, looking dishevelled, his skin pallid, and he's shivering.

"What the heck Cody. What's the matter?"

"You need to come and see this, it's amazing!"

He drags me by the hand up the stairs to our bedroom. He approaches the mirror and places his hands on its surface.

"Watch this," he says.

He walks through the mirror and vanishes. A few minutes later, the front door opens and closes, and I hear Cody's footsteps running up the staircase. He bursts into the room.

"Did you see it?" Cody asks.

"Yes, I did," I remark, a bit abruptly.

"You don't look shocked. You already knew about the mirror, didn't you?"

"Yes I did, but I didn't want to concern you. I don't think we should be messing with this anymore. I went into town this afternoon to see the man at the store, but the place is shut down, like it's been that way for years, and we were only there a couple of weeks ago."

"Why didn't you say anything? You shouldn't hide things from me. I'll be downstairs if you need me. Right now, I'm too angry to talk to you," he says, stomping off.

I go over to the mirror and put my hand against it, but it's solid.

I run myself a bath and have a nice long soak to calm me.

After I'm done, I go downstairs to talk to Cody, but I can't find him anywhere. I check outside and the car is gone. I venture back to our bedroom, and the mirror has gone too. *Did he take it away?* Several hours later he returns. He's startled when he sees me sitting in semi-darkness in the living room.

"Hell! You gave me a fright," he says.

He walks into the kitchen, pours a glass of wine, then he sits down at the dinner table.

"Where have you been?" I ask sullenly.

"I got rid of the mirror, it's dangerous! I've been at the library researching them, and what I learned is very frightening. It's a portal of some kind," he says, taking a long gulp of his drink.

"A what? What's a portal?"

"Well, in some culture's mirrors are considered to be gateways to other realms and dimensions. Spirits can become trapped inside the mirror, while others have the ability to come and go as they please. Apparently, you're supposed to cover them so entities can't use it. I think we messed up babe. I dumped it. I left it under the overpass. If someone wants it, they can help themselves. It's not our problem anymore."

"Okay. I agree you did the right thing, but you could have told me. How did you lift it, when it took both of us to move it?"

"Weirdly, it wasn't heavy at all. It was light to carry actually. Anyway, it's late, and I'm bushed. Let's go to bed."

When we enter our bedroom, the mirror is standing against the wall.

"Omigod! I swear I got rid of it. I don't get it!" Cody says, plonking down on the bed, heavy with burden.

I'm staring at the mirror because inside it I can see a group of figures in black sitting in a circle. They're chanting and singing in a language I can't comprehend. Cody doesn't seem to see them. As if by some unseen power, I'm pulled towards the mirror. I touch the glass and my hand goes through it.

"Should we try it out just one more time?" I ask without waiting for an answer.

I walk into the mirror, right into the middle of the circle of people. They're wearing black cloaks, and they have their faces covered by a thin veil – I can't see their features. I look back and I see Cody watching, but he doesn't come through the mirror.

They all converge on me, and I scream in terror as I'm thrown to the ground, knocking my head on a rock.

I come to, on a cold concrete floor. The air is stagnant and smells putrid. I'm in a tiny room lit by several red candles. The cloaked figures stand around watching me intently. Their faces are wrinkled with old age – they look ancient. Sulphur burns my nostrils and stings my eyes. There's a gilded mirror on the wall across from me. I see Cody, and he looks frantic. He's knocking on the mirror screaming my name over and over. I yell at him to help, but he doesn't seem to hear me.

Eventually, the spirits of the mirror leave me, and they walk away. I hear the door lock behind them. Cody is holding his hand up to the glass. I go over and touch it.

"Helen, I can see you, please come back, I need you!" He sobs.

"I can't. I'm stuck in here and I don't know what to do," I cry.

Cody says hello, and that he loves me, every morning before he sets off for the day. He comes to me at night, crying, and looking lost and forlorn. We can touch the glass, but I can't feel his skin against mine, and it makes me sad. I watch as the years pass by. Overtime, he ages. He visits me less and less. One day he stops coming all together. Until he puts the mirror on the backseat. When he drops it off at an antique shop, I cry and shriek for him not to do it. But it's too late, he walks away.

I never see Cody again, as the years sweep by. The mirror sits in the store for several years. I wish I could go back in time, undo it all. I want my old life back. I watch people come up and inquire about the mirror, but nobody buys it. The store closes down when the owner eventually dies.

Everything is sold off, except for the gilded mirror. It sits in a storage unit for decades, with me trapped inside. Until one day, by chance, it breaks, and I'm released into the spirit realm.

# The House on Broken Hill

It's a cold wet winter's day. Amanda sits on the soft white leather couch in the psychologist's office. Lamps spread a warm amber glow around the room. She's curled into a ball hugging herself tightly, biting on her fingernails, ripping them off with her teeth, as she talks about the haunted house she grew up in on Broken Hill.

"The first time I saw Nail Head, I was about six years old," she says with hesitation as she grips the couch with white knuckles. "Mum turned out my light, and I fell into a deep sleep. A shrieking sound ripped me from my dreams, plunging me into a nightmare. There he was, Nail Head. I couldn't move, I was literally frozen to the spot. He was staring right at me...he...oh my god, he was standing on the ceiling, hanging upside down with his face right next to mine. His eyes were black and soulless. Poking out from his head were nails of all different sizes. I told myself I was still dreaming, he wasn't real, but I could feel his breath against my cheek, and the smell from his mouth was so putrid, like decay and rotten meat; I nearly vomited. Then he ripped his mouth apart with his hands...oh god this is too hard...I can't do this. I've been having nightmares again doc, they are really scaring me! And I don't know if this is real or all in my head."

Dr. Wilson pulls his chair closer and pats her hands to loosen the knots.

"Ok, ok...look, just calm down. Take deep breaths; you're safe here in my office, nothing bad can happen to you here, I promise. I'll get you a glass of water, you need a break. Be back in a minute."

Dr. Wilson leaves the room, rubbing his temples where a headache has formed. He's unsettled by Amanda and her tall tales, it's a lot of information to process. He assesses that she must be hallucinating, or perhaps she has some type of psychosis. She's been coming here for a couple of months, and this is the second time Amanda has mentioned this entity she's named Nail Head. As he makes it to the kitchenette his spectacles are fogged up and he can't see two steps in front of him. But he sees something. A shadow?

It passes him and disappears into his office. He quickly whips off his glasses, wipes them on his shirt and looks back, but there is nobody there. Moments later, he returns to his office with a glass of water, and finds Amanda sitting at his desk.

"Amanda, are you okay?"

He slowly steps towards her, and when he sees her up close, he drops the glass in shock; it shatters on the ground, making a dreadful sound. A scream breaches his mouth. Her eyes are closed tight, and her mouth is open unnaturally; it's ungodly! Ribbons of black veins are popping up all over her face. She looks dead, but he takes the chance to feel for a pulse. He reaches for her wrist. She's deathly cold as his fingers settle there, he feels no pulse. Abruptly, she grabs his arm and screeches like a banshee – it is so intense that he has to cover his ears. He watches on transfixed, as all the windows in the office implode, sending shards of glass across the room.

Suddenly she stops, closes her mouth and upon the floor she crumples. He proceeds to do CPR, while his secretary calls for an ambulance. After some time, Amanda's eyes fly open and her colour slowly returns. She sputters and takes in great gulps of breath.

"What happened?" she asks.

He never did answer her question. He ran from the room, passed his secretary, out the door of the building, into his car, and he never looked back. That was the day Dr. Roman Wilson quit his job, and his life changed forever.

Five years later, Amanda is in Roman's car as they travel to the house on Broken Hill. Roman is now a paranormal investigator. Since he discovered the truth about the unknown and unseen; Amanda's story has been ruminating inside his mind for years.

In fact, it was due to what took place in his office that prompted him to change the trajectory of his profession. From doctor to ghost investigator is quite a huge leap. He'd contacted Amanda again to finish off where they had begun years before.

When finally, they arrive at the house, it still looks the same to Amanda. Nothing much has changed, except the trees are taller and the garden is overgrown. Her father always kept the gardens in pristine condition; it saddens her – all his hard work had been for nothing. They stand on the wraparound porch, and Roman pulls the keys from his pocket. He puts it in the lock.

*The key enters the hole and the building feels it – it groans in anticipation. After being somewhat lonely for the past few years, it remembers the feeling of being full, then empty.*

*It senses immediately that someone has returned from eons ago, though it isn't sure who it is, just yet.*

The door screams and creaks as it is opened. Ahead of them, there is only a maw of darkness; the sun has not entered here for years. Roman turns on the light, it is dim, then it blinks out.

"At least the power is still on. Perhaps some of the bulbs need replacing?" he says mainly to himself to explain the light bulbs sudden extinction.

They make their way towards the back of the house. He hears a noise above them, like someone is softly walking, he ignores it and carries on regardless. Roman hadn't noticed that Amanda has stopped dead in her tracks, looking at a painting on the wall.

"This is a portrait of my parents. Why would they still have this up in the house after all of these years?" she asks, clearly baffled.

"Maybe they kept it up, you know, as a historical contribution? Didn't you say this house is two hundred years old?"

"Yes, something like that."

The kitchen is in darkness when they reach it.

"How about we go around and open these curtains? It's too dark in here," Roman remarks.

After going from room to room, letting light into the bottom floor, they sit at the dinner table.

"I'm going to record everything that happens while we are here," he explains. "I've brought a few devices with me.

I've got to go out to the car to get them, but I think we'll start with some backstory first. I'll record this on my cell phone and transcribe it later."

"Okay," she replies, as a floorboard above them creaks.

*The girl is back, the one who fled with her family. She is petrified, and so she should be. This house was never meant to be built. The graves beneath the property are full, and the ghosts inside them are restless. As are the spirits in the house.*

The house has been on the market for twenty years, and the real estate agent gave them permission to stay there for the weekend.

"I'll start our first session, okay? We've got this place for two nights, so there should be plenty of time to work through this," he says. Turning on the cellphone recorder he asks, "so, who did you live here with?"

"My parents and my older brother Matthew. I was about ten years old when we left this house for good," she answers.

"That must have been terrifying. Can you recall your first memory?" Roman asks.

"I was about four years old and I was out in the garden with mum and Matt; I think dad was at work. Mum was hanging washing. I lost sight of her because I was chasing butterflies, and I ran to the back of the property. There was an old man digging a large hole. I asked him what he was doing, and when he turned towards me, there was something wrong with his face.

It looked like he'd been in a fire, because his skin appeared to be melted. He said to me he was digging a grave. When I asked him who it was for, he said it was for me."

Amanda's face pales at the memory, and needles of anxiety crawl across her skin.

"What happened after that?" Roman prompts.

"I ran back to mum and told her about the old man and the grave, but she didn't believe me. I even made her come with me so I could show her, but when we reached the spot, he was gone, and there was no hole in the ground. She spanked me for lying."

Suddenly, they're interrupted by the sound of a loud crash coming from somewhere in the house. Roman's eyes search the room, but he says nothing about it. He tells himself they must have left the front door open and the wind slammed it shut.

*We take in the subtle change around the girl. Can she feel us watching her? There is movement from somewhere within.*

*Footsteps walking the hallway. The soft patter of tiny feet. It's the twins – they're up to no good.*

Roman reaches for his satchel bag he's slung over the chair. As he turns around, he's certain he glimpsed someone standing in the doorway. After everything he has documented over the past few years, of this, he is sure; ghosts are one hundred percent real. All of a sudden, the air around them turns bone chilling cold – like icicles are forming in the corners of the room.

"Something is in the house with us, I can feel it. I really think I should bring in my gear, set up and get this going. There is a pressure building; I feel it in my bones."

Roman's growing excitement makes Amanda feel uneasy. She wonders if this was actually a really bad idea coming back here.

Roman lives for the chance to prove the paranormal is real – he has done that a thousand times over. He stands, tightens his coat, and walks towards the door.

"I'm going to get my equipment so we can begin. Do you want to help me? I could use a hand."

"Sure," she replies.

When they get outside, the sun has left the property due to the large trees smothering the light. It's bitter cold, and the car has frost on it. Roman has a thought, they need to get some heating going and sort out the lighting. He doesn't want to be in the house, in the dark, no way! Not without proper electricity – it seems too temperamental to rely on. He grabs a heavy-duty torch and takes it inside with his equipment. Roman decides they will investigate the downstairs area first, and during the day they will focus on the upstairs areas. They dare not explore the upper floors at night.

*So, they are scared to come upstairs? Good. The old man in the attic is stirring. If he starts up, there will be no mercy. He will wake the man in the basement. Together they are lethal.*

Sitting around the table again, Roman spends some time showing Amanda the equipment, devices, and gadgets. She's never seen anything like it, so he explains their functions. Cameras and tripods, she recognises these. But there are cat ball toys, he calls them ghost detectors. Even a teddy bear that talks, it shocks her to no end. The one which fascinates her the most, is the SLS camera, which according to him indicates where an entity is in the room; they show themselves as stick figures.

"We'll start with this. It's an EMF device, a K2 meter, and it can detect energy in the room. If a spirit is near it will register by lighting up this box."

He places it on the dusty old oak table and turns it on. Suddenly, the lights begin to flash on the device, from green to yellow to red.

"There's someone here with us. Look at how the lights indicate their presence, isn't it amazing?"

"Yes, it is," Amanda replies; voice trembling.

"I'm going to use the spirit box to see if they want to talk." He pulls out a black box, with a small round speaker attached to it, and places it on the table. "This is an Ovilus device," Roman explains.

Roman switches it on and almost immediately a giggle bursts through the speaker. Then it scans through white noise, so loud and annoying to the ears, but Roman is used to it – heard it thousands of times. A deep guttural voice explodes through the nonsense chatter, but the words are illegible.

Night has entered the room, they shut the heavy red velvet drapes. Dislodged from the folds, dust motes float around the room like ghostly orbs.

"Spirits, if there is anyone here with us, could you please say your name? If you come up to this device in my hand, you can use it to communicate with us," Roman commands.

The spirit box rattles in his hand. For the life of him, he doesn't know why, but this house is different to any other place he has investigated thus far. This house is heavy with burden and lost souls, he can feel it in the energy around them. The device goes off, and another giggle comes through the spirit box.

"Did you hear that? It sounds like children. Do you ever remember hearing that when you were living here?"

"All the time, and I would see them too. They were small, and there were two of them; they looked like twins."

It's getting near midnight by the time they wrap it up. They decide to resume in the morning, after not much luck communicating with the dead. Roman chooses to spend the night on the couch. Amanda has made up the bed in her old bedroom, even though she is a little apprehensive about sleeping in that room again. Perhaps the ghosts will come calling? Do they know she is here? This might be the only time to face it head on; have some closure.

*The man in the attic has woken the man in the basement, they are walking around the bottom floor, where the girl is sleeping in her old bedroom. The twins are running around, up, and down the staircase. Nail Head has finally arrived.*

Roman wakes to an ear-splitting scream. When he opens his eyes, there are two men standing either side of the bed. One is wielding a long-handled axe, while the other man, who looks like he's been burnt in a fire, is leaning on a shovel.

At first Roman believes he is dreaming, but the REM pod on the bedside table is beeping, the red light sending a murderous blood red colour around the room. Someone must be playing with it. Giggles fill the air, followed by the soft patter of little feet running around the living room, and out into the hallway.

He sits up confused, and in fear he leaps to his feet. As he leaves the room, he grabs the flashlight, and he can hear heavy footsteps following close behind him, so he walks a little faster. Fear doesn't usually get the better of him, but right now his survival instincts are kicking in. He's too scared to look back as he flees the living room to check on Amanda.

The hairs on his arms prickle, warning Roman that something isn't right. The air is charged with energy. He bursts into Amanda's bedroom without bothering to knock. The room is ice cold when he enters.

"Amanda, you need to wake up," he yells.

He searches for a light switch in the darkness with trembling fingers. He flicks it on but nothing happens. The only light is the moon glowing through rips in the curtains. He doesn't want to scare her, so he keeps the torchlight off for now.

He makes his way over to Amanda.

"Amanda, wake up! We need to leave!"

Still no response; *the sleeping pills must have put her out for the night*. This isn't good, they need to get out of here. The two men are pacing outside the room, he can hear their heavy tread stomping along the corridor.

Roman finally grasps the fact they aren't human, they're ghosts, or more precisely, most probably demonic entities.

*Nail Head, he finally has her, after all of these years of waiting...*

Roman switches on the flashlight. The torch is flashing on and off, he has to hit it a couple of times to get it to work properly. He can hear scratching at the door, loud thumps and bangs are coming from the hallway. When he'd entered the bedroom, he had locked them in, but now the door is opening and slamming shut. Each noise has him jumping out of his skin. Terror consumes him whole. In desperation he shakes her legs. Still nothing. When the torch light finally shines across her form upon the bed, now he can see why she isn't answering him. His scream is choked off when Nail Head turns in Roman's direction. What Roman sees, stops his heart cold.

He falls to the floor, clutching his chest. Roman writhes in pain as he dies there upon the ground.

Nail Head has Amanda's head in his mouth. His jaw is stretched around her and all that is visible is half of her body, he has devoured the top half.

Standing in the room are the ghosts of the past. There are hundreds of them. They live here; this is their home. This is where they will spend the rest of their eternal lives, stuck inside the house on Broken Hill. No one will ever live here again – the spirits will make sure of it.

# Extreme Quarantine

At the very height of the pandemic, Roger has been in lockdown now for seven long gruelling days, in a quarantine facility in central Auckland, close to the Sky Tower, and it's driving him insane. He still has another week to go, and he doesn't think he'll last that long, being stuck in this stinky poky room with a single bed in one corner, a side table, an empty dusty shelf, and a painting glued to the wall; an ugly rendition of the Auckland harbour bridge.

The bathroom is the size of a closet, with a false mirror affixed to the wall. There isn't even a window. There are no electrical sockets, TV or Wi-Fi in the room, he feels as if he's in a prison cell. They took his cell phone off him when he'd arrived, and though they laxly searched him for drugs, alcohol, and weapons, they didn't find the kabar knife inside a hidden compartment in his backpack. Its handle is gold, in a black leather sheath. He knows he probably should've dumped it, he took a major risk, but he kept it just in case a golden opportunity were to arise. Plus, it's his favourite, and he carries it everywhere he goes. He brought it when he was overseas, on R & R in Afghanistan.

He's counting down the days until he's released, so he can continue where he left off satisfying his needs and desires. Roger wasn't permitted home to collect any clothes or supplies, when they nabbed him at a Covid check point.

They'd brought him here in a paddy wagon with a couple of other people. Upon arrival, they handed him a care pack, in it was a cake of soap, shampoo and conditioner; in little hotel room sized bottles, a toothbrush and toothpaste, a couple of shirts, hoodie tops, sweatpants, a pack of briefs and socks. It's a blessing and a curse that they let him keep his watch as it's the only way for Roger to track the passage of time.

Roger is crawling along the floor on his hands and knees, in a desperate state, as claustrophobia closes in. He reaches beneath the mattress for the knife, clasps it by the handle, and an intense feeling of desire shoots through his veins. He can't hold off any longer, the need, lust, thirst, is too great to ignore or suppress. He takes it with him into the bathroom, flicks on the bright florescent light, and peruses himself in the mirror; the surface distorts his features. He looks like crap.

His face, as it ripples on the surface of the artificial mirror, makes him appear cracked and hideous. He salivates thinking about cutting through flesh and bone. He misses the feelings it evokes. The voice inside his head, it's so loud and commanding, he's trembling. Sickness churns inside his gut when he comprehends that there is no alternative. He has to do it!

He can't go out and hunt because he's locked in 24/7 to stop the spread of the Coronavirus. Three times a day, two people come to the room to deliver food through a crack in the door, dressed in PPA gear. They shove in a fresh flannel and towel once a day, but they don't bother to take away the dirty ones. They're not good targets, he can't get his hands on any of them, they're untouchable, safety in numbers, and they're armed with tasers. He noticed all of this the first day here. If he had his arsenal with him, he'd have no problem obliterating them one by one. He did it when he was in the army, when they seconded him and his team into a special unit. He didn't even flinch when it came to annihilating the enemy. He's lethal with a knife, an expert when it comes to killing. It makes him the perfect serial killer.

Roger smashes his head against the mirror, trying to dislodge his overpowering impulses, and he doesn't stop until the room starts to sway. He wipes blood from his face with the back of his hand. Instant gratifying relief has him wanting more. So, he makes the decision and commits. Placing his hand on the rim of the sink, he severs off the pinkie finger from his left hand. With a wet mushy sound, it drops into the sink. His heart skips a beat. Then excruciating pain blasts throughout his core, like a grenade, rendering him momentarily immobile. In that moment, something within him snaps. It brings him to life. His breath erupts. An unbound awareness grips him.

He'd never thought in a million years that hurting himself would bring such unbridled pleasure. He drops to the floor unconscious.

When he comes to, bloody handprints mark the sink, and his hand feels like it's on fire or been run over by a freight train. He moans, but doesn't scream. Over the next hour, all five digits are completely removed from his left hand. He wraps the stump in a towel, it's filthy wet and it stinks. Roger drags himself along the floor, onto the bed, wanting nothing more than to sleep. But it's useless, he's too hyped up on adrenalin, thoughts a ruminating mess, too many emotions to grapple with. This new compulsion devours all of his thoughts. He needs more! Slowly rising to his feet, his head spinning, the room tilting, red streaks cover nearly every surface, he tries to calm his breath. Metal and salt permeate the air. He licks his lips, he's always loved that scent, if he could bottle it he would turn it into a cologne.

A knock on the door makes him jump out of his skin. It opens, food wrapped in a paper bag is pushed through the crack, the door slams shut; it's so loud it rattles his teeth. Every sensation is intensely heightened, he's never felt more alive in his entire life. He bolts to the loo and throws up. The intensity of the situation drives his fortitude. His mangled hand fascinates him to no end.

He's thrilled to discover how much more appealing his own blood looks compared to that of his numerous victims. This motivates him to carry on. He regains his strength and slowly he severs his left arm from the elbow down, leaving a bleeding mash of bone and matter. He passes out again. When he drifts back to reality, flat on his back, with the kabar lying on his chest, in his right hand, he clutches the globby mess of his detached left arm.

A scream finally explodes, but he smothers it by putting the dismembered arm into his mouth, and clamps down as hard as he can with his teeth. The taste of his own flesh stirs something dark and evil within him. His screams morph into diabolical laughter of pure absurdity, and tears of insufferable agony pour down the sides of his face. His face...his bulbous alcoholic nose.

In a clouded haze, he takes the knife and he expertly cuts through the bridge, all the flesh, gore, bits of bone, fall into the sink along with his other severed body parts. In the gore splattered mirror, the hole in the middle of his face makes him smile. Spread across the floor, bodily fluids make it slippery. He stumbles and cracks his head on the edge of the toilet.

When he eventually wakes, his enormous sense of achievement is short lived, he needs more, he's not quite satisfied yet. Looking down at himself, he's repulsed at the sight of his wrecked body. There are other parts that need to go. He doesn't look quite right. Something inside his head is broken. He ignores it all to continue on with his mission – satiating his need to mutilate and destroy. A sadistic urge is pulsating through his body, and though the suffering is all consuming, it's not enough to stop him. With the knife he continues. Even when it becomes blunt, he carries on regardless.

When the breakfast crew arrive the following morning, the vile stench emanating from the room stops them in their tracks. They call the authorities. The first cop to enter, throws up his eggs and bacon. The second cop is enthralled by what he sees, he freezes, horrified, yet intrigued.

One of the paramedics' faints, though her partner catches her before she hits the deck, right into a puddle of something that shouldn't be outside of a human body. They try to avoid the unmentionable globby bits and pieces, indistinguishable to the untrained eye. On the bed is the most horrendous scene – one to give them all nightmares for years to come. Roger is now a torso, with a nearly decapitated head, and his right arm is clutching the kabar knife. If that is not gruelling enough, he's missing his ears, nose, lips, and his only remaining features are two bulging bloodshot blue eyes.

# Dead or Alive

I'm on the run and hiding from the undead, they are the ones that I fear the most because I don't ever want to become one of them. I'd thought Zombies were only in the movies; how completely wrong was I. As far as I know I could be the last human being alive because I haven't come across any other living souls. All that is left is ungodly and atrocious.

What happened was that my brother Steve and I had been contracted by an obsessive explorer and some famous anthropologist to excavate a cave they believed to be hiding one of the gateways to Hell. For us it was an easy enough challenge. If someone was willing to pay for our expertise in caving, so be it. We did these types of gigs because we were interested in the unknown and the unseen. Hunting for treasures and getting paid for it.

You see, we were told where to find it and when we found the door with symbols above it, the feeling I got was that we should have got the fuck out of there. Instead, we opened it by bashing it in with a sledgehammer, and the sound of it cracking, and the pieces falling into the void, was shockingly violent and unexpected. What we did was carelessly and inadvertently unleash death and destruction, a deadly virus, and malevolent entities into the world.

Expelled from the gaping hole surged a glowing green fog that spread out and around us. It emitted an intense sulphuric stench that filled the air, making me choke and splutter. Outrageous cries bellowed around us, making my teeth chatter.

If it hadn't been for the fact I was attached by a rope as a green mass exploded out of the cave and out into the world, I would have plummeted to my death.

Through the doorway from where it came was an empty abyss of nothingness, and the sounds coming from within – I will never forget. Screams and wails of agonising torment nearly blew out my eardrums.

When we finally made it out of the cave, something chased us out, swooshing and galloping behind us as we fled for our lives. Outside, the fog weaved a pathway through the trees. As it dispersed above the river, its particles turned the water an algae green colour. When it reached the clouds, a sickly glowing hue disbanded across the sky. In a chaotic blur we packed up, jumped into our vehicles and abandoned the site.

It wasn't until the following morning that I realised something was terribly wrong. My bedroom was cast in a smoky green haze. Out the window, psychedelic colours burst across the sky – much like the Aurora lights. In a panic I rushed into the living room and switched on the TV. That was the moment I grasped the true aftermath of what we'd done. The sheer magnitude of our actions had me crumpled to my knees, sobbing at the scene on the television of total depravity and reckoning.

I couldn't turn my eyes away from the appalling images flashing across the screen. Guilt slithered through me like a venomous snake. If it weren't for us trying to unravel the mysteries of our world, this would never have happened. My stomach churned with bile at what we'd done. It was shocking to see how fast the devastation was spreading across the globe. Suddenly, the TV turned to static, followed by a public service announcement. It warned people to turn off all electronic devices; though, they never explained why. We were told to stay inside our houses, and not to leave until further notice.

I had to call my parents to see if they were okay. However, when I made the call, a maddening guttural scream exploded down the line. It was piercing enough to raise the dead from their eternal slumber. An electronic beeping and an electric shock had me dropping the cell phone to the ground. Then, the radio on the counter switched on by itself.

A priest was harping on about the end of days. These bizarre occurrences had me freaking the hell out.

After pulling out the radio plug, I rushed around the house switching off all the devices. I'd come to realise that whatever it was we'd set free from the gateway had infested the power and the electronics. I knew I'd have to turn off the electricity completely, if I were to remain safe. Hesitantly, I opened the backdoor and rushed out to the power box, switching it off.

Feeling slightly relieved, I made my way back to the house.

As I did, I got this creeping sinking feeling that I was being watched. Abruptly and without warning, something flew at me, knocking me over. It swooped down with a thunderous roar, picking me up with giant talons. Somehow, I managed to struggle free from its grasp, landing hard on my back, knocking the wind out of me. Breathless and in a state of shock, I watched the skies. Large, winged creatures that looked like giant Vultures, some with people in their giant jaws, ripping them apart mid-air, with their humongous claws, soared through my neighbourhood. I ran inside and from the window I watched them.

I knew the time to abandon ship had come. If I was going to survive, I needed to get to my bunker in the woods, where I'd be safe, and out of reach of the creatures, the ghastly ghouls, and the malicious green fog.

I'd been prepared for the Apocalypse for several years. When the twenty-first century approached, and with all the fear mongering associated with Y2K, my two brothers and I built a bunker into the woods, about fifty meters from the house.

After midnight I left the relative safety of my home for the bunker. The sky was still glowing green, and now it was sparking blue and yellow, like it was alive with electricity. It was denser than it had been initially, which had me worried about breathing it in. This gave me the incentive to run faster. My body ached, my knees weak. I wanted to give in. But I kept going. As I tore through the bush, to the sounds of clomping footsteps pursuing me, I was terrified.

The bunker was in sight, when all of a sudden something grabbed my leg, and I face planted into a puddle of ghastly green sludge. As it dragged me along the ground, I screamed out in intolerable pain as its claws dug into my flesh. Fading in and out of consciousness from the knock to my head when I fell to the ground, I managed to push myself up and punch it hard in its scaly face. It screeched and dropped me.

With adrenalin pulsing through my veins, I got up and I sprinted the rest of the way.

In haste I entered the code on the padlock, pushing the little buttons I hadn't felt in nearly twenty-five years. I scrambled into the bunker, to the sound of wings flapping, and an ear-piercing shriek. I made it inside and locked myself in. After locating the candles and matches; fortunately they still fired, I lit several, dispersing some of the shadows. We never did work out getting power. I cried. Trembled. Taking deep breaths to calm my nerves. My head was a confusing mess of emotions. Realistically, I'd no supplies because we never got around to stocking it properly. We lost interest after we built it; realising it would cost an arm and a leg to continue.

If it was night or day I could not tell.

After what felt like forever, but was probably only a day, I decided to go outside. When I opened the hatch I was surprised to see the green fog had completely dissipated. I could hear birds singing and chattering in the trees. Under a deep cerulean sky, and with the sun shining bright, warming my face, deeming it safe enough, I decided to go home. When I reached the front door it was standing ajar. Silently I pushed it open.

Upon hearing noises coming from somewhere inside, I moved slowly through the house. When I entered the kitchen, I couldn't believe what I was seeing. Sitting at my dining table were five Zombies in a state of utter shambles. Their skin was peeling off their faces, blood and other matter soiled their ripped clothing. I could tell they weren't alive people because their skin was the colour of the dead – grey and marbled. And the sounds they made were truly petrifying. As a pack, they turned and chased after me as I fled the house.

I thought I could outrun them, but they have super speed. And now I am dying because one of the fuckers bit me! If anyone finds this, I'm either dead, or one of the undead.

# About the Author

Del Gibson lives in Wellington, New Zealand. She is an author of dark paranormal horror fiction, as well as non-fiction works. Gibson has 40 short stories published by Reedsy Publishing. Gibson has also had her short horror stories published in several horror anthologies; Flash of the Dead, The Flash of Fangs, Wicked Flashes of Fantasy, Flashes of Nightmares, Apocalypse Tales: The End is Nigh, Flash of the Dead: Requiem, Flash of the Undead, and Merry Creepmas:

The Green book, published by Wicked Shadow Press, in both eBook and paperback. Gibson also contributed a short story to, Remains to be Told, published and edited by New Zealand multi-award-winning author and 6-time winner of the Bram Stoker award, Lee Murry. This anthology won the Sir Julius Vogel award for Best Collection in 2024, and which Gibson was nominated for the Sir Julius Vogel award, for Best Short Story. This is available in eBook and paperback.

She also has a short story featured in the anthology, HORRORific Tales: Hauntings, Volume 1, released in 2024, and edited by Colin Martin. Gibson was a recipient of a scholarship with Storied Imaginarium, run by American author Carina Bissett. She is the executive producer and writer for a short film, Undying Love, released on March 12th, 2025. Gibson also is one of the producers of the feature film, The Actor's Curse: A Tale of Twisted Fate, which is currently being filmed, by American filmmaker Phil Herman.

She also enjoys being an independent film reviewer of horror films (independent and mainstream.)

Gibson has a YouTube channel where you can find all of her film reviews, interviews with people in the independent film horrorsphere, and where she teaches writing tips. Gibson runs a popular Facebook group called, HORROR CENTRAL, where she currently has 44 thousand plus members. She also has another Facebook group, where you can find all of her published works, DEL GIBSON WRITING GROUP.

Embark on a HORRORific journey with our anthology series
HORRORific Tales
Volume One (Hauntings)
HORRORific Tales
Volume Two (Cryptids)
HORRORific Tales
Volume Three (Serial Killers)

Printed in Dunstable, United Kingdom

63662038R00127